➢ George Sullivan

TREASURE HUNT

The Sixteen-Year Search
for the Lost
Treasure Ship *Atocha*

FLORIDA CLASSICS LIBRARY • PORT SALERNO, FLORIDA

1993 second printing by agreement with the author.
Florida Classics Library
P.O. Box 1657
Port Salerno, Florida 34992-1657
Library of Congress Cataloging-in-Publication Data
Sullivan, George
Treasure hunt.
Bibliography: p.
Includes index.
Summary: Describes the historical background,
the frustrations, false trails, lawsuits, and eventual
success of the long search for a sunken Spanish
treasure ship lost off the coast of Florida.
  1. Nuestra Señora de Atocha (Ship)—Juvenile
literature.   2. Treasure-trove—Florida—Juvenile
literature.   [1. Nuestra Señora de Atocha (Ship)
2. Buried treasure]   II. Title.
G530.N83S85   1987   917.59′41   87-8791

Designed by Victoria Hartman
Jacket photo and interior
on-site photos by Pat Clyne
Printed in the United States of America
10 9 8 7 6 5 4 3 2 1

ISBN 0-912451-30-0

Acknowledgments

This book would not have been possible without the constant cooperation of company officials, archaeological consultants, boat captains, and divers representing Treasure Salvors, Inc. Special thanks are due Mel and Deo Fisher, Bleth McHaley, R. Duncan Mathewson, John Dorwin, Jim Sinclair, Don Kincaid, Pat Clyne, and Fay Feild. Thanks are also due Tony Kopp, Tom Ford, Ralph Budd, Sandy McKinney, Curtis W. E. White, Judy Sojourner, Don Jonas, R. D. LeClaire, Taffi Fisher Quesada, and Kathy Simpson; also, Carol Shaughnessy, Charles Garrett, Garrett Electronics, and Franca Kurti of TLC Custom Labs.

Contents

TREASURE HUNT

Underwater metal detectors helped to pinpoint the location of the *Atocha* treasure. (CEDAM International; Rick Sammon)

1

Sunken Treasure

A board the salvage boat *Dauntless*, anchored in the Gulf of Mexico about forty-one miles west of Key West, Florida, Saturday, July 20, 1985, was a day like most others—hot, almost windless, the green sea calm.

On deck, two divers, Andy Matroci and Greg Wareham, strapped on their diving masks and cylinder-shaped oxygen tanks, then jumped feet first into the open sea. Kicking with their flippers, they quickly made their way downward through the warm water—ten feet, twenty feet, thirty, forty. An electronic reading aboard the *Dauntless* had indicated a pile of what could be metallic material on the ocean floor. Matroci and Wareham had been assigned to check it out.

Visibility was good. At about fifty-five feet, Matroci spotted ancient silver coins scattered about the ocean bottom. He fanned some of the sand away from the coins with his hands. More and more coins appeared.

Wareham, meanwhile, flippered ahead. He held a metal detector in front of him. Suddenly what appeared to be a large mound of coral crawling with spiny lobsters loomed up. When Wareham passed the detector over the mound, the machine screeched so loudly that he almost dropped it.

Crew members haul a load of seventy-pound silver bars to the deck of the salvage boat *Dauntless*. (Pat Clyne)

The coral-covered mound turned out to be nearly solid silver: a stack of hundreds of silver bars, each the size of a loaf of bread, and many thousands of silver coins.

Wareham waved Matroci over to take a look. The two men stared at timbers that looked like part of a ship's hull, with the mound of silver sitting on top. The divers hugged one another, then raced for the surface. They popped out of the water with their fists raised in triumph. Matroci screamed the news to the crew members of the *Dauntless*. "It's here! It's the main pile! We're sitting on silver bars."

The "main pile," also called the mother lode, discovered that summer day, turned out to be the biggest cache of sunken treasure ever found. Before the year ended, divers had recovered almost 1,000 silver bars, each weighing about seventy pounds, and some 140,000 silver coins. They also found 315 emeralds.

And they found gold—bars and disks, coins and jewelry. The sea ruins almost everything—except gold. Even gold that had rested on the ocean bottom for three and a half centuries shone brightly when found. Some of the gold looked like it had just come from a jewelry-store window.

Thirteen-year-old Torin Kublik displays gold bars he found at the *Atocha* site. (Pat Clyne)

Altogether, the gold, silver, and jewels were worth about $150 million. The treasure represented the climax of a sixteen-year search for the wreckage of the Spanish galleon *Nuestra Señora de Atocha* that sank in a hurricane in 1622.

The quest for the *Atocha* proved to be much more than a successful treasure hunt. The vessel itself has enormous historical importance. Archaeologists have scoured the site, measuring and photographing, recording and analyzing. "Finding the *Atocha* was like finding a huge time capsule," says R. Duncan Mathewson, chief archaeologist on the project. "It's as important as Pompeii or King Tut's tomb."

The search for the *Atocha* was led by sixty-two-year-old Mel Fisher, a former chicken farmer from Hobart, Indiana. Fisher had been fascinated by treasure hunting ever since he had read the novels of Robert Louis Stevenson as a schoolboy.

After he moved to California, Fisher became interested in underwater diving. He used the money he made as the owner of a dive shop to finance his treasure-hunting expeditions.

Fisher would be the first to admit that underwater treasure hunting is never easy. There is more to it than anchoring over a sunken vessel and sending divers down to bring up the riches. For every treasure recovered, there are dozens of well-planned, well-executed attempts by professional divers that fail.

Fisher himself had to overcome the enormous financial burden that goes with buying salvage boats, equipping them with electronic search gear, and hiring divers. Several times Fisher hovered over the brink of bankruptcy.

He also faced serious legal problems with the state of Florida and the federal government as to who would finally own the treasure. Although Fisher eventually won the legal battles, he spent almost as much in lawyers' fees as he did paying divers and equipping boats.

There was personal tragedy, too. The discovery of the mother

Mel Fisher led the long and often difficult search for the *Atocha*. (Pat Clyne)

Some of the close to one thousand big silver bars recovered at the *Atocha* site. (George Sullivan)

lode came exactly ten years to the day after Fisher's eldest son and daughter-in-law drowned when their salvage boat sank. A diver died with them.

"At times we were close to quitting," said Fisher's wife, Deo, not long after the mother lode was found. "But if we had quit, we would have been miserable the rest of our lives."

Then she added, "If you have a dream, go for it."

Although there are great hazards involved, tremendous costs, and day-to-day frustrations, there is no shortage of adventurers who hunt for sunken treasure. And there is treasure to be found: many hundreds of seventeenth- and eighteenth-century ships met disaster on the sandbars and sunken coral reefs off Florida's southern coast.

The Spanish vessel *Atocha* was one such vessel, lost at sea on September 5, 1622, en route home from Havana, Cuba, with the wealth of the New World crammed into her holds and storerooms.

Over three hundred years later, in June 1970, Mel Fisher organized his search for the *Atocha*, triggering one of the most extraordinary adventure tales of modern times. It is a tale of danger and frustration and sacrifice; of false trails, disappointments, and great personal tragedy. "Sometimes we doubted our

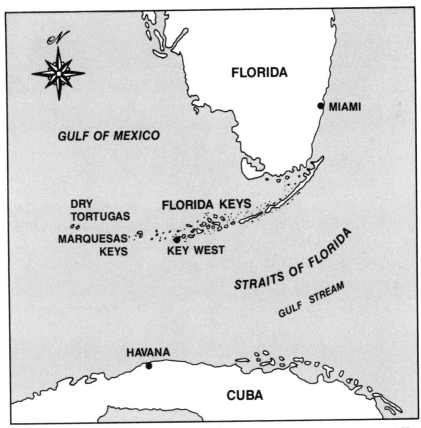

Remains of the *Atocha* were found off the Marquesas Keys west of Key West, Florida. (Map depicting lower Florida, the Keys, Marquesas Keys, Dry Tortugas)

Much of the *Atocha* treasure is now on display at Mel Fisher's headquarters in Key West, Florida. (George Sullivan)

ability to survive," an associate of Fisher once said.

But Fisher did more than merely survive—he won. He found the long-lost galleon and its golden treasure. He followed his dream to the end of the rainbow.

2.

Ship of Doom

F our hundred years ago, Spain was a superpower, as influential in world affairs as the United States or the Soviet Union are today.

The vast Spanish empire included the western fringe of South America and nearly all of the West Indies—the islands that are now Cuba, Puerto Rico, Haiti and the Dominican Republic, plus many others. Spanish possessions also took in Central America, Mexico, and what is now the southwestern United States.

As early as 1555, both Mexico City and Lima, Peru, had populations of over one hundred thousand, making them bigger than Seville and Toledo, the largest cities in Spain at the time. As for Boston, Philadelphia, and New York, the chief cities of colonial North America, it would be another half a century and more before they would even be founded.

The great period of Spanish expansion and conquest began with Christopher Columbus. Sailing in the service of Spain, Columbus became, in 1492, the first European to reach Latin America.

When he returned to Spain in March 1493, proclaiming that

he found "the Indies," Columbus created great excitement in Europe. Explorers representing several nations began probing the shores of North and South America.

John Cabot, an Italian navigator, commanded a voyage from England to North America in 1497. A Portuguese explorer named Pedro Álvares Cabral landed on the coast of what is now Brazil in 1500. Amerigo Vespucci, from Italy, made three voyages to South America from 1499 to 1504. (In 1507, a German mapmaker suggested that the "New World," as it was called, be named "America" after Amerigo Vespucci.) Columbus himself crossed the Atlantic again in 1493, 1498, and 1502, exploring what is now Jamaica, Puerto Rico, Trinidad, and the coasts of Panama and Venezuela.

In 1513, another Spanish explorer, Vasco Núñez de Balboa, led an expedition across Panama, the narrow strip of land connecting North and South America. He thus helped to prove that the New World was a separate land mass between Europe and Asia.

Spain was more aggressive than the other European nations in establishing its rule in the New World. From the first settlement that Columbus established on the island of Hispañola (now the republic of Haiti and the Dominican Republic), the Spanish expanded their claims to other islands and the mainland of Central America and South America.

Hernán Cortés landed in Mexico and by 1521 had conquered the Aztec empire, forcing the Indians to give up a fortune in gold and other riches. Francisco Pizarro's target was the wealthy Inca empire of what is now Peru. By 1535, Pizarro had brought Peru under Spanish control. He founded the city of Lima, which was to serve as Peru's capital and the center of Spanish government in South America.

Once in control of an area, the Spanish sought to exploit its natural resources. Colonists were granted huge tracts of land to grow sugarcane, tobacco, coffee, or cotton. Indian slaves were forced to farm the land.

Other colonists concentrated on the continent's mineral wealth, its silver and gold, diamonds and emeralds. For decades, the Spanish conquerors simply seized whatever gold and silver they wanted. Later, the Spanish enslaved the Indians to work the mines.

Silver came from many places, but no source was as important as the mines of Potosí in the central part of what is now Bolivia. There more than ten thousand Indians toiled from dawn to dusk in dimly lit, poorly ventilated mine shafts, digging the silver-bearing rock. They were paid pennies a day. Sometimes the Spanish paid the Indians in coca leaves, which they chewed. Coca contains the powerful and addictive drug cocaine. Whether they received coca leaves or money, the Indians were forced to labor; no one could refuse to work.

Mining the silver was not the worst of it. Other Indians hauled the ore to refining areas where the crushed rock was treated with a mixture of mercury and brine. Mercury is a deadly poison. Constant contact with the silvery liquid caused countless Indians to sicken and die.

Each year the slave labor at Potosí produced a great flood of coins and ingots. In one form or another, Spanish silver circulated freely throughout South America, and was in common use in Europe and known even in the Orient.

The riches of the New World were vital to Spain in maintaining its position as the most powerful nation in seventeenth-century Europe. Trade with the colonies followed a well-established system. Two fleets a year were sent to the New World. On the outgoing voyage from Spain, the vessels were laden with manufactured goods to be sold in the colonies. On the return voyage, the ships were filled with silver and gold, and with agricultural products: coffee, cotton, sugarcane, and tobacco.

Spanish fleets sailing for the New World followed much the same route that Columbus had taken. They would head south

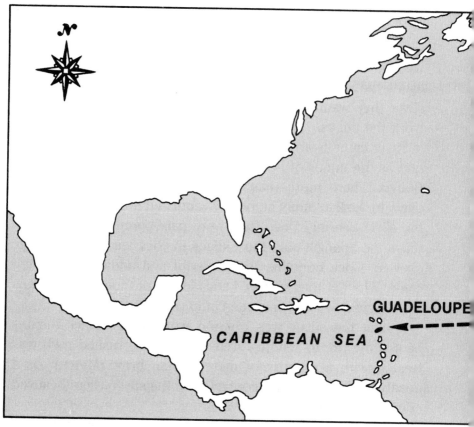

Route of the Spanish ships to New World ports.

from Spain toward the Canary Islands off the northwest coast of Africa. Somewhere south of the Canaries they would make a ninety-degree turn to the right, catch the easterly trade winds, and cross the Atlantic on about the latitude of the Caribbean island of Guadeloupe.

Early in the 1600s, conditions in Europe forced the Spanish to begin to provide armed ships to guard their fleets of merchant vessels. Spain had been drawn into the Thirty Years' War, which had been launched by Ferdinand II of Germany against the French to restore the Catholic religion to the German states. The Spanish supported Ferdinand. While the war went well from a military standpoint, it caused a great drain on the

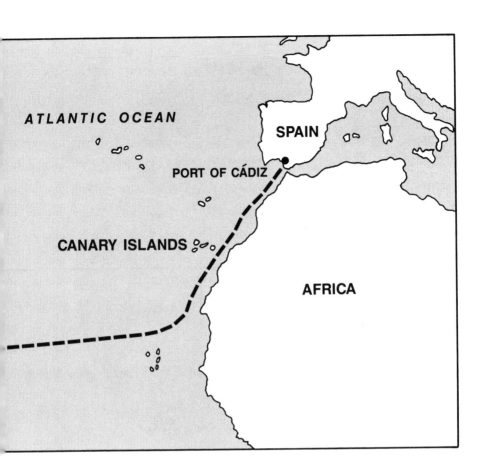

ATLANTIC OCEAN

SPAIN

PORT OF CÁDIZ

CANARY ISLANDS

AFRICA

Spanish treasury. Indeed, the war, plus wasteful spending, had put Spain on the road to financial collapse.

Besides the war with France, there was also trouble with the Dutch, who were expanding into areas where the Spanish had established colonies. In 1621, the year that Philip IV, a teenaged king, ascended the Spanish throne, Spain and Holland ended a long truce. That meant that Spain's merchant ships would be open to attack from the Dutch.

So it was that two heavily armed guard galleons were ordered to sail with each major fleet. One of them, to be known as the *capitana*, was the lead ship of the convoy. The other galleon, called the *almiranta*, was to bring up the rear.

PHILIPPES IV ROY DESPAGNE De Naples, de Sicile &c. Archiduc d'Auftriche.
Duc de Bourgongne, de Brabant, de Milan &c. Conte de Habsbourg, de Flandres &c. Fils du
Roy Philippes III et de Marguerite d'Auftriche Nafquit l'an 1605. Efpoufa en pr. nopces Elizabeth de Fr
ance Fille du Roy Henry le grand 1615. morte a Madrid 1644. apres auoir doné un fils a l'Efpagne mort 164
et une fille en qui reluifent fes vertus. Et en 2 nopces Marie Anne d'Auftriche fille de l'Emp. Ferdinand III. Au
comencem de fon regne il remporta diuerſ auantages fur les Hollandois fur mer, aux Indes, et au Palatinat.
La querre luy ayant eſté declareē en Flandre par le feu Roy 1635. le bon heur de la France et la mauuaiſe admi
niſtmon du Comte d'Oliuareʒ ſon pr. Miniſtre luy cauſa la perte de pluſieurs Villes en ces prouinces, en Italie et
en Efpagne; des prouinces et des Royaumes entiers. La Catalogne et le Portugal en 1640 ſe ſtans ſouſtraits de
ſa dominaoñ, le Royaume de Naples ayant couru le meſme danger en 1647. Mais comme l'eſperance des Ef
pagnols eſt inuincible, meſme au fort de leurs diſgraces; ils ont heureuſem' recouure une bonne partie de
leurs pertes, toutefois auec peu de gloire puis que ceſt par les diuiſions dont la France eſt agitee depuis
4 annees.

Philip IV became king of Spain in 1621, a year before the *Atocha*'s doomed voyage. (New York Public Library)

In 1616, officials of the Spanish crown arranged with Captain Alonso Ferrera to construct four guard galleons at his shipyard at Havana, Cuba. Ferrera agreed to have the ships completed by July 1619.

Each ship was to be 110 feet in length, thirty-three feet in width, and draw fourteen feet of water. Each was to carry square sails on its mainmast and foremast. The shorter mizzenmast was to be rigged with a triangular sail, a lateen. A long spar, or bowsprit, jutted from the upper end of the bow.

The tail end of each galleon was to be crowned with a tall sterncastle. There many of the ship's passengers would be quartered. The sterncastle and the towering masts made each of the galleons top-heavy. Even when loaded with cargo and passengers, the vessel had a tendency to rock scarily from side to side. To compensate for its top-heaviness, each ship carried ballast. This consisted mainly of heavy stones, some as big as basketballs, which were placed in the lower regions of the ship. The ballast helped to assure that the vessel would ride low in the water, making for greater stability.

Each of the vessels was fitted out with from twenty to twenty-four bronze cannons. Most of these were mounted on the gun deck, which was one deck below the open weather deck. Each ship also came equipped with five large anchors, one smaller anchor, and a full set of sails and rigging.

Ferrera completed the construction of the first three galleons by August 1619, missing his deadline by a month. But he was very late with the fourth galleon. This vessel, like many Spanish ships of the time, was given a holy name. It was christened *Nuestra Señora de Atocha,* "Our Lady of Atocha," in honor of a shrine to the Blessed Virgin to be found in Madrid. The vessel was provided with a small statue of Our Lady of Atocha and a likeness of the Virgin was painted on the ship's sterncastle.

Perhaps because he was behind schedule with the *Atocha,* Ferrera hurried the construction of the ship. A recent study of the *Atocha*'s timbers, recovered from the ocean bottom, has shown that the vessel was carelessly built. "She was thrown together," archaeologist R. Duncan Mathewson says. "That's one reason the ship sank the way it did."

Ferrera substituted mahogany for oak in some of the beams. When under great strain, oak has some "give" to it; it bends. Not mahogany; it breaks.

Ferrera also contributed to the *Atocha*'s destruction by skimping on nails and spikes. In nailing together some of the important beams, he was supposed to use five spikes but used only two.

"The ceiling timbers of the lower hull structure, which are also the lower deck timbers," says Mathewson, "were not even nailed to the main frames. They were just laid down."

Thus, a ship meant to survive the storms of the Gulf of Mexico and Atlantic Ocean was put together in a reckless manner. "The *Atocha*," says Mathewson, "was a ship of doom."

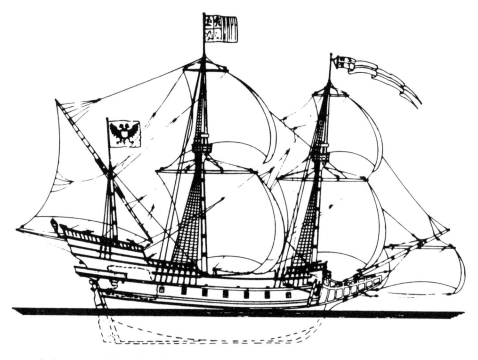

A drawing of the *Atocha* based on measurements contained in the original construction contract. (Treasure Salvors; Bill Muir)

From the beginning, the *Atocha* was dogged with bad luck.

On its first voyage, from Havana to Sanlúcar, a port city that served Seville, the ship's mainmast splintered, and the vessel had to return to Havana for repairs. On its second try, the *Atocha* sprang leaks in the bow, and more repairs were needed after the ship at last limped into port.

It was 1622 before the *Atocha* was ready to play the role for which it had been cast. Supplies for the voyage to the New World were loaded aboard the galleon early that year while the ship lay at anchor at Sanlúcar.

The *Atocha*, as a military escort, was to carry an entire company of infantrymen, eighty-two soldiers. Commanded by Captain Bartolemé García de Nodal, a noted explorer of the day, these men would defend the vessel in the event an enemy boarding party sought to capture the ship. Cases of muskets and barrels of gunpowder and shot went aboard with the soldiers.

The *Atocha*'s main holds were filled with bales of cloth, books, ironwork, barrels of wine, and large jars of olive oil. Three hundred cases of mercury, to be used in refining silver, were carried aboard. The last cargo loaded included the supplies for the voyage: biscuits, salt pork, vinegar, oil, honey, kidney beans, chickpeas, and water stored in casks and large jugs.

The fleet left Spain on March 23, 1622. Before its departure, the *Atocha* was designated the *almiranta*. She would thus travel as the rearmost ship of the convoy.

After crossing the Atlantic, the fleet stopped briefly at the island of Dominica in the West Indies, then continued directly west to Cartagena, Colombia, an important Caribbean port of the day. Some of the cargoes were unloaded before the ships sailed on to Portobello in what is now the Republic of Panama. There the fleet arrived on May 24, 1622.

3 ⤛

Disaster at Sea

O n July 1, the great Portobello Fair was to open. There, the cargoes brought from Spain would be sold and the ships loaded with silver and gold extracted from the New World mines. As the opening of the fair drew near, traders, sailors, and nobles poured into hot and steamy Portobello.

The *Atocha* and other ships anchored offshore. Cargoes were unloaded onto the barges that had been tied up to each ship and were then ferried ashore. The goods were stored in warehouses to await the start of the fair.

On the day the fair opened, the captains of the ships that made up the fleet met at the government house in Portobello with the captain-general of the guard fleet, Lope Díaz de Armendariz, Marquis of Cadereita, who had just arrived in Portobello.

Cadereita was becoming uneasy about the return voyage to Spain. Delays had already wrecked the original sailing schedule. What worried Cadereita was the hurricane season. While mariners of the day had no sophisticated weather-forecasting instruments, it was common knowledge that late summer was no time to be sailing the Caribbean or Gulf of Mexico. A West Indian verse put it this way:

June, too soon,
July, stand by,
August, come they must,
September, remember,
October, all over.

Cadereita knew that the ships must be under way for Spain by midsummer or disaster could occur.

During the captains' meeting, Cadereita learned that much of the silver that was to be loaded aboard the vessels for shipment to Spain had not yet arrived in Portobello. At Potosí, where it had been mined, refined, and cast into ingots, or bars, the silver had been packed onto the backs of llamas and hauled some one thousand miles to Callao, the port city for Lima. There the silver was loaded onto galleons. The galleons sailed north along the west coast of South America to Panama City on the west side of the Panamanian isthmus. Once the silver had reached Panama City, it was to be off-loaded for the trip across to the isthmus to Portobello.

But the silver intended for the *Atocha* and other ships was still in Panama City. That meant more delay. Cadereita immediately ordered the president of Panama to get the silver to Portobello as quickly as possible. Two days later, long processions of heavily laden mules began arriving in Portobello. They carried hundreds of silver ingots, each the size of a man's forearm and weighing between sixty and seventy pounds. The mule train also brought many thousands of silver coins.

Much of the silver, more than four tons of it, belonged to Philip IV. For the most part, it represented money that had been raised through taxes and fines.

Jacove de Vreder was the silvermaster aboard the *Atocha*. His job was to register each of the 133 silver bars as they were brought aboard. Not only were de Vreder's records meant to serve as the *Atocha*'s official list of cargo, they were also to be

One of the silver bars bearing the A and R stamp of Lorenzo de Arriola. (George Sullivan)

the basis for the assessment and collection of taxes.

Lorenzo de Arriola, a noted Potosí merchant, was to return to Spain aboard the *Atocha*, bringing with him sixty silver bars. Silvermaster de Vreder recorded the numbers and symbols that had been stamped into the surface of each bar. These included the bar's weight, its serial number, and the degree of silver fineness. In the case of Arriola, each bar was stamped with his mark: an *A* and *R* joined together, with a diamond above.

The document prepared by de Vreder stated that the silver would be turned over to Arriola in Seville, after he paid taxes and shipping charges. These terms were to be met, de Vreder's document noted solemnly, "if God brings the ship safely to Spain."

Martin Salgado went aboard the *Atocha* with his wife, Maria, their teenage daughter, and their servants. Salgado had been a government official in Lima. His wealth was represented by sixteen silver bars that he registered with de Vreder.

Salgado also brought aboard about forty pounds of silverware. These items included a large silver plate decorated with a coat of arms and two names, Salgado on one side and Saliere on the other. Also pictured on the plate were two houses connected by a chain and a pool out of which a pair of birds were drinking. This was a marriage plate, one that represented the joining of the Salgado and Saliere families.

Martin Jíminez was the navigator of the *Atocha*, the person responsible for plotting the course of the ship across the Atlantic. The big chest that Jíminez took aboard contained the tools of his trade: an ivory sundial, compasses, several sets of divid-

Archaeologist Jim Sinclair inspects silver plates, cups, and other artifacts recovered from the *Atocha*. (George Sullivan)

ers, and an astrolabe, an instrument used for determining the position of the stars.

But beneath the instruments, and concealed from the eyes of de Vreder and the king's tax officials, Jíminez had stored two gold chains, gold dust, gold nuggets, eight gold coins, and enough silver coins to fill eleven bags.

The navigator wasn't the only person involved in smuggling. "Gold was stashed all over the place," says R. Duncan Mathewson. It has been estimated that as much as one-quarter of all the gold carried by the *Atocha* and other Spanish vessels of the day was being smuggled into Spain in an effort to avoid the payment of government taxes.

When the Portobello Fair had ended and the silver and gold and other cargo had been brought aboard, the ships took on supplies and prepared to sail. Some forty-eight passengers went aboard the *Atocha* at Portobello. Most of them were men and women of wealth and education. Some were government officials who had served Spain in the New World and were now returning home. Others were merchants or traders. A handful were priests and church officials. With the passengers went a dazzling array of jewelry: rings, medallions, necklaces, brooches, and gold chains.

The names of the wealthy passengers and the government and church officials were entered on the ship's register. At least eight servants and slaves were also among the passengers. But since these eight were recorded as "persons of no importance," their names were not recorded.

On July 22, the fleet set sail from Portobello for a return visit to Cartagena. There additional treasure was brought aboard the *Atocha*, much of it gold. The registered cargo included more gold coins and dozens of gleaming gold bars and disks. Many of the gold items displayed the king's tax stamp.

More than five hundred bales of tobacco—about twelve tons

Gold bar bearing
an assortment of seals
and stamps. (George Sullivan)

of it—were also taken aboard the *Atocha* at Cartagena. When Columbus had made his first voyage to the New World, he had seen the natives smoking cylinder-shaped rolls of dried leaves, which they called *tabacos*. Spanish settlers tried smoking and enjoyed it. Before long, the use of tobacco spread across Europe, with the smokers supplied with tobacco from plantations that had been established along the coast of Colombia. It was from these plantations that the bales of tobacco loaded aboard the *Atocha* had come.

On August 3, 1622, the ships left Cartagena and sailed for the port of Havana, about one thousand miles to the north. There

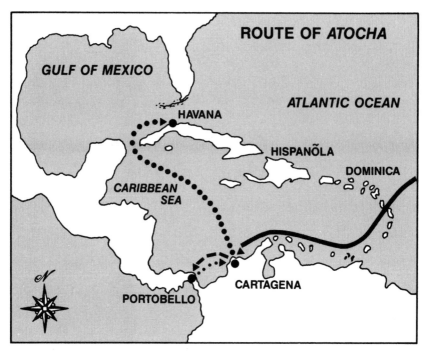

Route of the *Atocha* after its Atlantic crossing.

were many days with no wind to speak of during the voyage, which added to the fleet's delay. By the time the ships reached Havana, the hurricane season had begun.

There was more cargo to be loaded in Havana. The *Atocha* took aboard 582 copper ingots from the king's Cuban mines. Each ingot had been crudely formed by digging a shallow, circular hole in the ground and filling it with molten copper. The copper was to be used in the casting of bronze cannons.

Three hundred bales of indigo, a plant used in manufacturing blue dye, were also loaded. More gold and silver bars and coins went aboard, too.

By the time the *Atocha* was ready to sail, every available space was crammed with passengers or cargo. There were 265 people on board, plus live chickens and sea turtles for food. The treasure that had been recorded by de Vreder included 255,000 silver coins, 901 silver bars, and 161 pieces of gold.

By the last days of August, the twenty-eight vessels that were to make the Atlantic crossing were ready to depart. The Marquis de Cadereita met with the ships' captains to decide a departure date. They were now six weeks behind schedule. A deadly hurricane could strike at any time. Yet they had to sail; there really was no choice. With each day's delay, Spain's financial situation worsened. Only the valuable cargo aboard the ships could ease the pressure.

There were no scientific instruments for forecasting the weather in those days. Mariners relied, instead, on natural signs to predict what weather was coming. European sailors, for example, are said to have originated the rhyme that goes:

> Red sky in the morning, sailor take warning.
> Red sky at night, sailor's delight.

The wind and clouds were observed carefully. Wind out of the east was said to be "good for neither man nor beast." High-flying, fast-moving cirrus clouds were also thought to indicate bad weather.

Mariners also believed that the weather was greatly influenced by the movements of the planets. The lunar phase known as the new moon was considered especially significant. The earth and the moon were said to be "in conjunction" at that time. Whatever weather prevailed at the time of the new moon would continue for several days.

A new moon was scheduled for September 5 in 1622. The Marquis de Cadereita decided that if the weather on the day of the new moon was fair, the ships should sail. He felt they would thus be guaranteed several additional days of good weather— enough time for the convoy to thread its way through the treacherous waters of the Florida Straits north of Havana. This would assure the safety of the ships.

On Sunday, September 4, the sky was clear and sun-filled. If the day before the new moon could be so perfect, the Marquis reasoned, the next day would surely also be fair. He ordered the fleet to sail. The twenty-eight ships, their flags flying smartly, left Havana in single file. The *Atocha*, as the *almiranta*, was the last to depart.

The ships headed north toward the Florida Keys, the chain of small islands and coral reefs off of the southern coast of what is now the state of Florida. As the ships approached the Keys, which are about ninety miles from Havana, they would enter the Gulf Stream, the strong ocean current that flows north from the Gulf of Mexico along the east coast of the United States. The plan was for the ships to ride the Gulf Stream northward.

Keeping the coastline within sight, the ships were to head east and then north until they reached the latitude of their destination. Navigators of the seventeenth century did not have the instruments that permitted them to find their longitude, which is the angular distance east and west on the earth's surface. But they could figure their latitude, the angular distance north and south of the equator. And that was enough to keep them on course.

Cádiz, Spain, the fleet's destination, is positioned at approximately 36 degrees latitude. When the fleet reached roughly that same latitude off the North American coast, they would make a ninety-degree right turn, then run straight for Spain. It was simple but it worked.

The first day at sea was uneventful. But as night fell the wind out of the northeast began to grow stronger. It increased in intensity through the night, and by daybreak it was viciously lashing the fleet. Combing the surface of the northward-flowing Gulf Stream, the shrieking wind raised the seas to mountainous levels. The skies were dark. Heavy rain pelted down.

Aboard the *Atocha*, sailors lowered the mainsail to reduce the battering. Even so, the ship became harder and harder to control in the angry seas. As it rocked crazily, the ship's timbers shuddered and groaned. Sails and rigging were reduced to tatters. Anything not lashed down went careening about the decks, crashing into bulkheads.

Belowdecks, the uneasiness of the passengers had turned to outright fear. Many lay in their bunks miserably seasick. Some knelt in a group around the statue of the Our Lady of Atocha. The captain led prayers, his words often blotted out by the howling wind.

That night the wind shifted to the south. It drove most of the ships north and past the Dry Tortugas, a group of islands about seventy miles to the west of Key West at the entrance to the Gulf of Mexico. These vessels managed to ride out the storm in the deep waters of the Gulf.

The *Atocha* and a handful of other vessels at the tail end of the convoy, including the *Santa Margarita* and *Rosario*, were not so fortunate. The wind hurled them toward the dreaded coral reefs. Caught in the shift in the howling wind, the *Santa Margarita* lost her foresail, then her mainmast and the use of her tiller. The ship drifted helplessly in the churning sea, then began to break up. Sailors aboard the *Atocha* dropped the ship's anchor in an effort to check its advance toward disaster. But the anchor line snapped.

The wind pushed the *Atocha* closer and closer to the menacing reefs. A high wave lifted the ship, then sent it crashing down on a coral plateau. The reef ripped into the ship's bow and the sea poured through the gaping hole.

The *Atocha* sank quickly, pulled down by the weight of the sailors, soldiers, slaves and passengers, the stone ballast, the cannons and cannonballs, the many tons of silver and gold, the copper ingots, the tobacco and other cargo. The bow sat on the bottom while the top of the mizzenmast jutted above the surface.

When the sky cleared, the sun revealed the sea to be littered with boxes and barrels and splintered planks and masts. A small merchant ship, the *Santa Cruz*, made its way through the debris. When it got close to where the *Atocha* had sunk, lookouts aboard the *Santa Cruz* spotted survivors clinging to the ship's mizzenmast. There were five of them: a seaman, Andrés Lorenzo; two young apprentices, Juan Muñoz and Francisco Núñez; and two black slaves. Of the two hundred and sixty other people aboard the *Atocha*, all had perished.

The disaster that struck the treasure fleet sent shock waves through all of Spain. The loss of human life saddened many hundreds of families. Whole fortunes were wiped out. Countless merchants and traders faced financial ruin. The news of the loss sickened King Philip IV. His creditors began making dire threats. Finding the sunken vessels and recovering the gold and silver they carried became the number one priority of the Spanish crown.

Diver probes remains of the *Atocha* on ocean bottom. (Pat Clyne)

4

Vain Attempts

Within weeks after the *Atocha* and other ships had gone down, the Marquis de Cadereita launched efforts to salvage the wrecks. He assigned Captain Gaspar de Vargas, a seagoing veteran, to search for the ships. In mid-September 1622, Captain Vargas sailed from Havana for the Florida Keys.

When Vargas arrived at the spot where the *Atocha* lay, he measured the water's depth and found it to be 55 feet. Salvage divers in those days stayed at the bottom for only as long as the air in their lungs lasted. And although diving to the bottom in 55 feet of water is no easy matter, Vargas's divers were able to inspect the *Atocha*'s hull. But they were unable to break into it and salvage the treasure because the hatches were tightly secured.

Vargas's men also searched the area where they believed the *Santa Margarita* had gone down but found nothing. They then moved farther to the west, to the Dry Tortugas. There they found the *Rosario*, which was stranded in shallow water so it was relatively easy to salvage her valuables.

Vargas planned to return to the *Atocha* after he had obtained the tools and explosives that would enable him to crack open the hull. Before leaving, he marked the site with a buoy.

But Vargas never got the chance. A second hurricane—even more powerful than the first—ravaged the area, tearing the *Atocha* apart. When the vessel sank, it went down bow first. Much of the cargo and ballast shifted to the bow as the vessel settled.

The second storm tore loose the *Atocha*'s upper hull and decks. But the timbers that formed the lower hull section were pinned to the ocean floor by the tons of ballast, silver bars, and copper ingots.

The upper portion of the ship was carried to the northwest, scattering barrels, ballast stones, cannon balls, weapons of various types, coins, gold bars, and pieces of jewelry and pottery along the way. The heavy load of cannon was finally deposited some seven miles from the lower hull section.

When Captain Vargas returned to the wreck site, his heart sank. His buoy and the *Atocha*'s mizzenmast had disappeared. Vargas could now only guess at where the hull lay.

Vargas established a camp on one of a group of small, nameless islands, each of which was blanketed with a thick growth of mangrove, not far from where he believed the wreck might be. Every morning, he would be rowed out to the site to supervise his divers. Sometimes the trip took several hours.

The standard salvage method of the day involved suspending a long cable between two small boats. Grappling hooks were hung from the cable, which was weighted down with cannon balls. As the two boats were rowed along parallel courses, the cable was lowered and the grappling hooks would sweep the ocean floor. Anytime a hook snagged something, a diver would be sent down to investigate. Vargas and his men toiled for weeks in vain.

The Marquis de Cadereita was upset by Captain Vargas's lack

of success. In February 1623, he left Havana to join Vargas, setting up camp on the same small island that Vargas occupied. To honor his distinguished visitor, Vargas named the cluster of islands in the Marquis's honor, calling them the *Cayos del Marqués*, that is, "Keys of the Marquis." (A key is a low offshore island or reef.) Today, these islands, located about thirty miles west of Key West, are known as the Marquesas Keys.

Marquesas Keys sit low in the water, about twenty-five miles west of Key West. (Pat Clyne)

Cadereita stayed at the site for about a month. During that time, divers recovered two silver bars and a chest of silver coins. But that was all.

Cadereita returned to Havana in the spring, still hopeful that the missing treasure would be found. But his hopes were never realized. Several feet of sand drifted over the wreck site, frustrating the efforts of Vargas's divers. That summer he abandoned the search.

The next man to try to salvage the *Atocha*'s treasure was Francisco Núñez Melián, a politician and adventurer from Havana. Melián got salvage rights to the sunken vessels through a contract with Philip IV. It provided that the king would get one-third of any recovered treasure, one-third would be awarded to Melián, and the remaining third would go toward paying the expenses of the expedition.

Melián believed he had an advantage over ordinary underwater treasure seekers of the time—and he did. Melián's edge was a 680-pound diving bell that he had invented. It was shaped like an upside-down cone and could be lowered from a boat on the surface to the ocean bottom.

The device worked on a simple principle. When you press an upside-down drinking glass into a pail of water, air gets trapped at the top of the glass. Even when the glass is fully submerged, the air remains inside. When Melián lowered his diving bell into the waters of the Gulf of Mexico, the air was similarly trapped. A diver supported by a platform within the bell breathed the trapped air.

In 1626, Melián brought his diving bell to the site where the *Atocha* supposedly sank. He spent a month looking for the wreck without any luck.

Melián then moved his operations to an area several miles to the northwest where the *Santa Margarita* went down. There he enjoyed great success. On June 19, 1626, one of his divers spied the wreckage of the *Margarita* as the bell was being dragged along the bottom. Before the summer was over, Melián had raised 313 silver bars, a mass of silver coins, and many other items of silver.

Melián posted an auditor, Juan de Chaves, in a boat on the surface. The divers working the site were instructed to bring the handfuls of coins they recovered to Chaves, who counted and sorted them and saw to it that they were deposited in a chest on the salvage ship. Not all the divers were honest, Chaves soon learned. He found some of them trying to hide coins in the boat. He discovered other coins in divers' pockets. Chaves then ordered all divers' pockets to be cut off in an effort to stop the thievery.

Melián continued to work the *Santa Margarita* site for four more years, although his efforts were sometimes interrupted by Dutch warships. The treasure he recovered made Melián rich and famous. The king appointed him governor of Venezuela. Melián died in 1644.

After the death of Melián, salvage efforts faded. In 1688, the Spanish House of Trade, which regulated commerce in the New World, published a list of sunken vessels. The name *Atocha* was at the top of the list.

Decades passed. New kings came to power in Spain. Other treasure ships were smashed by hurricanes or victimized by pirates. In 1715 and again in 1733, whole fleets of ships were lost in storms off Florida's east coast. These disasters helped to wipe out memories of what had happened to the *Atocha*.

During the 1700s, Spain and Great Britain challenged one another for colonial power in America. The British destroyed Spanish missions in Florida, but in 1783 Spain was granted Florida by treaty.

Early in the next century, Spain lost many of its colonies. A

Lone pencil buoy marks the spot in the Gulf of Mexico where remains of *Atocha* lie.

new power, the United States, rose to confront the Spanish. After Andrew Jackson led an American invasion of Florida in 1818, the territory was ceded to the United States. Congress established a territorial government in Florida in 1822.

Through the centuries, the battered remains of the *Atocha* rested on the ocean bottom in waters off the Cayos del Marques. If any man could find the *Atocha*'s treasure, it was his. But it remained untouched.

When the *Atocha* went down, the ship's register and the records kept by silvermaster de Vreder went to the bottom with it. But copies of these and other documents had been made. One set of records eventually found its way to the Archives of the Indies in Seville. There the records were wrapped in folders. The folders were tied in bundles with heavy ribbon. Whoever opened the bundles and read the documents would be put on course for the *Atocha* and the golden treasure the ship contained.

5

First Steps

How many golden galleons besides the *Atocha* were sent to the bottom by ferocious storms and Florida's coral reefs is anybody's guess. A person swimming north along the Florida Keys and up the East Coast might come upon a sunken galleon every quarter of a mile or so. And the coastline stretches hundreds of miles.

Until fairly recent times, the methods used to explore sunken vessels and salvage what treasure they might contain were very primitive. Spanish salvors in the New World enslaved Indians and blacks to scavenge the wrecks. Clutching rocks to their bellies to overcome their buoyancy, these divers were able to go down as far as 150 feet. A diver in those days stayed down for only as long as he could hold his breath.

Through the years, there were countless efforts to develop diving helmets or hoods that worked on the same principle as the diving bell used by Francisco Núñez Melián in salvaging treasure from the *Santa Margarita*. Air was supplied to the diver on the bottom through a hose from a hand pump or bellows on the surface.

The invention of the air compressor early in the nineteenth

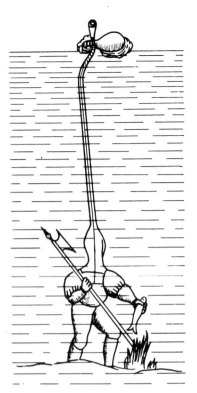

This early diving "hood" dates to A.D. 375. (New York Public Library)

century led to the development of a more practical diving system. It was the work of a German-born engineer named August Siebe, who has been called the "Father of Commercial Diving."

Siebe outfitted the diver in a metal helmet that was attached to a waist-length metal jacket. Air was pumped to the helmet from a compressor on the surface. Any excess air forced into the helmet, along with the air that the diver exhaled, was allowed to escape at the bottom of the jacket.

When using this system, it was vital that the diver stand up straight at all times. If he tilted forward or back or to either side, the jacket and helmet began to fill with water—with disastrous results.

In 1837, Siebe took his invention a step further. The diver wore the same metal helmet, which was now fitted with intake and outtake valves, and the helmet was connected by a hose to

The deep-sea diver of the early decades of the present century wore a heavy metal helmet and rubberized suit. Surface pump provided air through a long hose. (New York Public Library)

an air compressor. But instead of having the diver wear a metal jacket, he enclosed him in a flexible watertight suit.

This system, with little change, was used by so-called deep-sea divers throughout the early decades of the present century. They wore rubberized canvas suits, screw-on brass or copper helmets that weighed as much as sixty pounds, eighty-five-pound lead belts, and heavily leaded boots. A surface pump provided air through a long hose.

Hard-hat divers, as they were also called, played an important role in the construction of tunnels and bridges. They became well known for their exploits in rescuing crew members trapped in sunken submarines and for their work as salvage divers.

But the equipment they wore was really not well suited for underwater treasure seeking. It was too heavy, too clumsy. It was also very costly.

A breakthrough came in 1942. That year a French naval lieutenant named Jacques-Yves Cousteau, working with an engi-

Jacques Cousteau, working with engineer Emile Gagnon, developed the first practical underwater breathing system. (ABC-TV)

neer named Emile Gagnon, developed the first practical self-contained underwater breathing apparatus, or scuba.

With scuba, the diver carries one or more tanks of compressed air on his back. He or she breathes through a mouthpiece connected to a regulator by an air hose. The regulator provides the diver with a constant source of air at the right pressure. Exhaled air is allowed to escape into the water through the regulator.

Scuba, when combined with a face mask and a pair of flippers and, for cold-water diving, a protective wet suit, opened the underwater world to millions. Virtually anyone with the proper training could dive and search for treasure.

During the late 1940s, the first scuba-equipped divers began invading the reefs off the Florida Keys to find coins of silver and gold and valuable artifacts. News of these finds spread rapidly. By the beginning of the 1950s, the excitement of underwater treasure hunting caught many thousands in its grip.

Mel Fisher, the man who one day was to find the *Atocha*, was one of the first to learn about scuba. Underwater diving had always fascinated him. At the age of twelve, he had experimented with a primitive diving helmet, one that he fashioned out of a five-gallon paint can. It was fitted with a glass window made watertight at the edges through the use of lead caulking that Fisher had obtained by melting down his toy soldiers.

Fisher was supplied with air that came from a bicycle pump that a friend worked at the surface. The first time Fisher tried out the helmet, the window popped out because the friend pumped too furiously. Fisher almost drowned.

Fisher studied engineering at Purdue University and served with the Army Engineers in France during World War II. Landing there not long after D-Day in June 1943, Fisher was assigned to repairing and rebuilding what had been destroyed in battle. He first saw scuba being used in French coastal waters.

When the war ended and he was a civilian again, Fisher

Scuba gave the diver freedom to roam the underwater world without having to depend on a supply of air at the surface. (Bahamas Ministry of Tourism)

returned to the United States. He couldn't decide what to do with his life. Restless, he drifted from one city to another. He lived in Chicago for a time, then Denver, then Tampa, Florida. There he bought some scuba equipment and tried his hand at spearfishing. He soon became a very skilled diver, earning a reputation as a young man who brought in bigger fish and more of them than anybody else.

Fisher also began taking underwater photographs. As he once told a friend: "Some people wouldn't believe my stories about the huge fish I speared, so I took photographs of them to prove my stories were true."

One day at the St. Petersburg City Pier in Tampa Bay, a diver showed Fisher some interesting objects that he had recovered from the ocean bottom. These included an ancient padlock and key, some pieces of pottery, and a few silver coins. They represented the first Spanish treasure that Mel had ever seen. He never forgot that moment.

In 1950, Fisher moved again, this time to California. He and his father went into the chicken-raising business. They built a chicken ranch in Torrance, in the Los Angeles area. Although he now had some ten thousand chickens to worry about, Mel couldn't forget his diving experiences in Florida, and he soon began diving regularly in the Pacific Ocean.

One thing bothered Fisher and his fellow divers. They had to drive a long distance to the shop where they got their air tanks refilled. Fisher solved this problem by buying an air compressor and installing it in the feed shed of the chicken ranch. The compressor enabled him to fill his own tanks and those of his friends. When other divers found out about the service, they, too, began turning up at the ranch to get their tanks refilled.

Before long, Fisher's dive shop, one of only a handful then in operation, was becoming very profitable. No other ranch enterprise earned as much money. Fisher next built a machine shop and began manufacturing spear guns, masks, snorkel breathing tubes, and other equipment.

Soon chicken raising became a thing of Mel's past. His father put the ranch up for sale. The Hortons, a family from Montana, wanted to buy the ranch. That's how Mel happened to meet sixteen-year-old Dolores Horton, nicknamed Deo. Mel and Deo fell in love. They were married in June 1953.

Mel taught Deo how to scuba dive. The beauty of the underwater world thrilled her. For their honeymoon, the couple went to Key West, Florida, on a diving expedition. A Key West fisherman directed them to the wreck of the *Balbanera*, a steel-hulled freighter that had been grounded off the Marquesas Keys in the 1920s. Mel and Deo made several dives through the warm, clear waters to the wreck site.

Mel was not seeking treasure. Spearfishing and underwater photography were his chief interests then. He and Deo had never heard of the *Atocha*. They had no idea that their quest for the Spanish treasure ship would one day lead them back to the Marquesas Keys and the very same waters where the *Balbanera* rested.

When the Fishers returned from Florida, they moved their dive shop closer to the Pacific Ocean, to Redondo Beach, also in southern California. Mel's Aqua Shop was what they named it. Not only did Mel fill air tanks and sell all kinds of equipment from spearguns to surfboards, he also launched a scuba-diving school. Thousands of students signed up for Mel's three-day course.

Bleth McHaley, who worked for *Skin Diver* magazine, and who later became a valued associate of Fisher's, recalls Mel from these days. "Mel was 'Mr. Skin Diver,' " she says. "He was a very big deal."

Deo was always Mel's working partner. But she had less time for diving and the dive shop as the Fisher family grew. In 1954, Dirk was born, and in 1955, another son, Kim.

Little by little, Mel's interest shifted from spearfishing and underwater photography to searching for sunken treasure. He formed a salvage club and bought a fifty-five-foot boat to take the club members out to known shipwrecks. He named the boat the *Golden Doubloon* after the gold coin the Spanish had used in the New World.

After Mel Fisher had achieved worldwide fame as a treasure hunter, someone once asked him to name the reason for his success. He said it stemmed from "an ability I have had to gather a group of specialized people around me and inspire them to make an all-out effort to succeed."

One such person was an electronics wizard named Fay Feild, who Fisher met during this period. Feild had invented a magnetometer, a highly sensitive, torpedo-shaped metal detector that could be used underwater.

The magnetometer is based on the principle that the earth's magnetic field is fairly constant in its intensity, except when it is disturbed by a concentration of iron or iron-based metal. When the magnetometer was towed behind a boat, an electronic receiving device in the boat's pilothouse would record on graph paper any magnetic variation it detected. A diver would then be sent down to find what caused the variation. It could be an anchor, a cannon, cannonball, nail or spike, barrel hoop, or even a musket ball—anything made of iron or lead. Whatever the object happened to be, it might lead to the site of a sunken wreck.

Feild's hobby, collecting rare spiny oyster shells, was what led him to develop his magnetometer. Spiny oysters are almost always found clinging to the hulls of sunken ships. Feild knew that with a magnetometer he could find lost ships, and thus spiny oysters. Commercial magnetometers were too expensive to buy, so Feild built his own.

Feild needed a boat from which to try out his invention. He looked in the Yellow Pages of his telephone directory and came upon Mel Fisher's name as the owner of the *Golden Doubloon.* "I called and asked Mel if he would take me along on one of his

Fay Feild poses with the magnetometer that found the *Atocha*. (George Sullivan)

trips so I could test my magnetometer," Feild recalled. "He didn't mind at all and he wouldn't take any money for it."

There were problems with the first magnetometer that Feild built, but eventually he got the device to perform better than commercial models. It was able to take as many as ten readings per second. This feature enabled Fisher's boats to travel at relatively high speeds during searches, at speeds as high as twenty knots (about twenty-two miles an hour). This, in turn, enabled the boats to cover wider expanses of ocean.

Fisher was at first content to do his treasure hunting off the California coast. But little by little he was lured to the waters of the Caribbean Sea, where richer wrecks lay. Fisher eventually concentrated on a site in the West Indies north of the Dominican Republic known as Silver Shoals. His target was a Spanish ship that had sunk in 1641.

In June 1960, Fisher loaded the *Golden Doubloon* with diving gear and search equipment and headed south from San Pedro, California, along the west coast of Mexico, and through the Panama Canal. While still in Panamanian coastal waters, and not far from Portobello, which had been a stopover for the *Atocha* and the 1622 treasure fleet, Fay Feild's magnetometer pinpointed a wreck. It proved to be a Spanish vessel.

When Mel went down to investigate, he saw cannons resting on a pile of ballast. He and his divers recovered nails, musketballs, and pottery from the wreck. But they found no silver or gold.

Mel's money ran out and he was forced to return to California before diving at Silver Shoals. But his appetite had been whetted. He had seen his first Spanish wreck. He knew he would return to the Caribbean soon.

6 ⤛

Another Step

Mel mapped out plans for a second expedition to Silver Shoals in 1962. On his way there, he stopped in Florida to see Clifford ("Kip") Wagner, the head of a group of treasure hunters who had been working several sites off Florida's Atlantic coast.

The name of the group was Real Eight. The word *real* (pronounced *ray-ahl*) is well known to treasure seekers. It is the name of a Spanish coin, about the size of a silver dollar, that was widely circulated in Spain and Spanish America during the seventeenth century. Eight reals equaled a peso, another Spanish silver coin of the period—the one familiar to anyone acquainted with pirate lore as a piece of eight.

Kip Wagner's interest in treasure hunting had been triggered by his hobby, which was beachcombing. After severe storms had raked the shoreline near Vero Beach, Florida, and rearranged the sand, Wagner would often find Spanish silver coins. One thing he noticed about the coins was that none was dated later than 1715. From copies of documents he was able to get, Wagner learned of a fleet of ten Spanish ships that had been driven into the reefs and shore not far from Vero Beach in 1715.

Obviously the coins he was finding had come from that fleet.

Working on weekends and holidays, Wagner and some of his friends had found several of the sunken wrecks, one of which yielded a number of wedge-shaped ingots of silver. In 1960, Real Eight had obtained a contract from the state of Florida that granted the company the search and salvage rights for a forty-mile stretch of coastline that extended south all the way from Sebastian Inlet (which is about forty miles south of Cape Canaveral) to the town of Stuart.

During 1961, Wagner's divers made several notable discoveries. The most exciting was a cache of several hundred silver coins. These represented the first sizable treasure discovered in Florida in more than a century.

Wagner was interested in expanding his group and asked Fisher whether he cared to join it. Mel would have to support himself in Florida for a year, pay his expenses, and divide anything he found with Real Eight on a fifty-fifty basis. In return, Mel would be getting the rights to work a site where important treasure was almost certain to be found.

Mel didn't agree to become a member of the Real Eight team right away. He still had Silver Shoals on his mind. But after his expedition there proved unsuccessful, Mel decided to pull up stakes and move to Florida to join forces with Kip Wagner.

Mel did not plan to do this on his own. He formed a group of divers and other specialists who were willing to give up their regular jobs and take a gamble on making treasure-hunting their chief occupation.

In the summer of 1963, Mel sold his home and his boat and leased his dive shop. He and Deo and the children packed their belongings into their car and a rented trailer and headed east. The Fisher family had continued to grow. Nine-year-old Dirk, a skilled diver, and seven-year-old Kim had been joined by Kane, who was three, and Taffi, the only girl, nearing her second birthday.

Once they were settled in Florida, Mel and the other members of his group bought a boat, installed their equipment aboard it, and went to work in an area that Kip Wagner had assigned to them. They found a silver wedge that summer, but little else.

One problem that the divers frequently faced was poor visibility. The remnants of the 1715 treasure fleet were buried in deep sand. Not only was removing the sand difficult, but any efforts to do so made the water very murky. Sometimes divers' visibility was reduced to inches: A hand outstretched in front of one's face was difficult to see.

To remove sand from the bottom, divers used a suction pipe called an airlift. A pump on the dive boat fed compressed air through a long hose into the lower end of a metal or plastic tube held by the diver.

The airlift worked something like a vacuum cleaner. As the compressed air expanded and sought to escape at the top of the tube, it created suction at the tube's bottom. Water would rush in, sucking with it sand, shells, and other small objects. This "overburden," as it was called, was ejected a few feet from the area being worked by the diver.

The diver would usually work facedown in the water, clutching the airlift tube under one arm and raking sand and other material toward the opening with the other hand. The diver would filter the sand through his fingers as he worked, feeling for coins or other worthwhile items. He also shunted aside large rocks that might possibly clog the tube.

The airlift was efficient enough. Its failing was that on any given dive only a relatively small patch of the bottom could be covered, particularly if the sand layer happened to be very deep. Worse, the airlift, by stirring up the sand, made for poor

Diver working with an airlift in waters off the Marquesas Keys. (Pat Clyne)

visibility. Even the biggest objects were blacked out.

Mel was well aware that the water at the surface was almost always crystal clear. How could he get that clear water down to his divers? Mel's inventive mind kept trying to provide an answer to that question.

One day, Mel discussed the problem with Fay Feild, whose magnetometers Mel was using. Feild quickly made a sketch of a device that he believed might represent a solution to the problem.

Mel bought some sheet metal and hammered it into shapes that resembled Feild's sketches. The result was a pair of elbow-shaped tubes that he mounted at the stern of a dive boat. When the boat was anchored over a spot where the divers planned to work, the tubes were swung down to enclose the boat's propellers. The other end of the tube then pointed straight downward. The idea was that when the propellers were turning they would drive the clear water at the surface down to the silty bottom. Mel called the device a mailbox.

Mel tried out a pair of mailboxes on a shipwreck near Fort Pierce. The water was about fifty feet deep. When the dive boat was in position over the wreck, its propellers spinning and the mailboxes in place, Mel went into the water to see how they worked. At the bottom, it was so murky that it was like being in a dark room. Mel and the divers watched as the propellers began forcing a column of clear water downward. At the bot-

A pair of mailboxes in a raised position. When they swing down, one end encloses the boat's propellers. (George Sullivan)

Mailboxes, also called blowers, force surface water downward, digging a crater in the ocean bottom. (Pat Clyne)

tom, the column slowly expanded into a huge bubble of clear water. Suddenly Mel could see the entire wreck, thousands of fish, and the ocean floor stretching in every direction. It was as if someone had switched on a light.

Then one of the divers noticed that the mailboxes were producing another benefit. They blew aside an enormous quantity of sand that covered the wreck site. As they continued to force water downward, they created a huge crater on the bottom.

The mailbox appeared to be more important than anyone could have dreamed. It did, in fact, bring sweeping change to the way the divers worked underwater. As Robert Daley noted, before the mailbox, divers were "like men working with shovels." What they needed was a bulldozer. The mailbox, in terms of what it was able to accomplish, had a bulldozer effect.

Fisher had revolutionized underwater treasure hunting. And he kept refining his technique. The first step was to locate a potential site with a magnetometer. Once the site had been established, it was pinpointed more accurately by divers using handheld metal detectors. If the object causing the magnetometer and detectors to react couldn't be spotted by the divers and appeared to be deeply buried, the mailboxes were brought in to blow the sand away. After they had done their work, divers with handheld detectors went down again to scan the sides and bottom of the crater that had been opened by the blast from the mailboxes.

The following year, in May 1964, while operating off Fort Pierce, Fisher and his divers used the technology to make one of the most spectacular finds in the history of underwater diving up to that time. The magnetometer had led to the discovery of an iron cannon, and near the cannon divers recovered ballast stones and more than one hundred silver coins.

On May 24, Fisher anchored a dive boat over the ballast pile, lowered the mailboxes into place, and switched on the props.

Divers went down. They were stunned by what they saw. The ocean bottom was littered with gold coins. The sand had been blown away exposing a carpet of gold.

The first diver to reach the surface screamed out, *"Gold!"* Within a minute, everyone from the boat was in the water.

They scooped up handfuls of coins, flippered their way to the surface, tossed the coins on the deck, then went back down for more. Fisher, grinning broadly, watched the divers. Then he found himself unable to resist the lure. He plunged to the bottom and began gathering up gold as frantically as everyone else.

That day, Fisher and his divers recovered 1,033 gold coins. Before they left the site, more than 2,700 were found. It is believed that the coins had come from a wooden chest that had rotted away, leaving the coins strewn about the ocean floor.

Hand-held metal detectors are brought into use after the magnetometer has pinpointed a site. (CEDAM; Rick Sammon)

The magnetometer and mailbox had proved to be of enormous value. And they would do so again and again in the years that followed.

By the end of the 1964 diving season, Real Eight divers had recovered more than a million dollars in treasure from the rotted remnants of Spanish ships. Their finds included, besides the gold coins, heavy ingots of gold and silver, thousands of silver coins, silver dishes, delicate pieces of porcelain, and magnificent jewelry.

These finds triggered a boom in Florida treasure hunting. Divers by the hundreds descended on the state, eager to repeat what the Real Eight divers had accomplished. In 1966 alone, forty-seven companies applied to the state of Florida for permits to salvage sunken treasure.

The great rush to hunt treasure in Florida's coastal waters created a serious problem. Some of the treasure seekers, in their eagerness to find gold and silver, dynamited and otherwise destroyed underwater wrecks. Or they simply looted sites, removing objects that might provide clues to the history of the sunken vessel.

To prevent the destruction of historical wrecks, the government of Florida tightened regulations concerning underwater treasure hunters. They were now expected to give up whatever they found to state inspectors and agree to yield twenty-five percent of their treasure to Florida as its share.

The new regulations didn't seem fair to Mel and his colleagues. They argued that if it weren't for their efforts the treasure and historical artifacts that rested in Florida's coastal waters would be lost forever.

The battle lines were drawn. In the years that followed, Fisher and his associates would be involved in a constant struggle with Florida, and later the federal government, over ownership rights to recovered treasure. The United States Supreme Court would eventually decide the issue.

7

Vital Clue

M el Fisher had heard of the *Atocha* and other sunken vessels of the 1622 Treasure Fleet before he moved to Florida. And once he was settled in Vero Beach and had begun working with Real Eight, he learned more about them.

Some of what he learned came from the *Treasure Diver's Guide*, a list of many sunken wrecks with the location of each. The *Guide* had been compiled by John S. Potter, Jr., a treasure hunter and shipwreck historian. Published in 1960, it was "must" reading for every Florida treasure seeker.

About the *Atocha*, the *Guide* said: "Over two million dollars in gold and silver went to the bottom off Alligator Reef when the New Spain armada's *Nuestra Señora de Atocha* was swamped and sank, taking down with her Admiral Pedro de Pasquier and nearly her entire crew. She settled at a depth of ten fathoms (sixty feet), then too deep for salvage. The treasure should still be there, strongly inviting."

Mel didn't need John Potter's guidebook to tell him that the *Atocha* and its treasure were "strongly inviting." The ship was becoming his main interest. He realized that it could be the "big hit" he was looking for.

Mel ended his connection with Real Eight in the late 1960s.

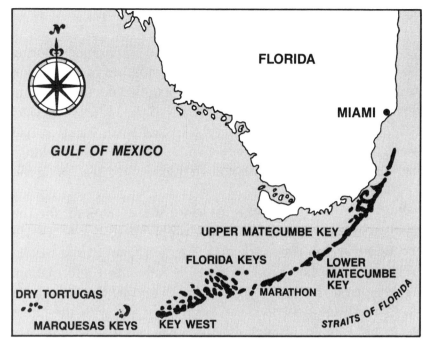

Florida Keys, lower Florida and Straits of Florida depicting Upper and Lower Matecumbe Keys, Marathon, and Key West; Marquesas Keys and Dry Tortugas.

After he and his associates had formed a group called Treasure Salvors, they obtained search and salvage rights from the state of Florida that covered the waters in the southernmost part of the state. Mel moved his operations to the Florida Keys and began searching for the *Atocha* on a full-time basis.

The Keys are a chain of small islands and reefs that stretch south and west on a sweeping curve for more than a hundred miles off Florida's southern coast. Spanish explorers, looking for a safe route through the Straits of Florida, landed there early in the sixteenth century. Through the years, pirates often used the Keys as a base of operations, hiding in the countless coves and channels the islands offer.

When Mel Fisher arrived there late in the 1960s, the Keys were bustling with treasure hunters. One of them was Art McKee, a treasure seeker since the late 1930s. Using a hard-hat rig, McKee had found enough cannons and other objects during the 1940s and 1950s to open a treasure museum on Plantation Key. Mel learned that Art McKee had obtained documents concerning the *Atocha* from the Archives of the Indies in Seville, Spain. One of them listed every gold and silver bar that had been carried by the vessel, along with the identifying markings for each. McKee had also obtained information describing the location of the ship.

Burt Webber was another treasure hunter looking for the *Atocha*. Webber had been making preparations for years. He had underwritten the work of a research team at the Seville archives, which had produced a large amount of information. Webber planned to carry out his search aboard the *Revenge*, a 136-foot salvage boat that had been fitted out with the latest electronic equipment, including an advanced magnetometer.

Webber, McKee, and Fisher, and anyone else interested in locating the *Atocha*, were aware that the documents in Seville referring to the 1622 ships described them as being lost in "the Keys of the Matecumbe." There was no secret as to where the Keys of the Matecumbe were located. Every tourist who has driven along the Overseas Highway (U.S. 1) that links the Keys to one another and to the southern tip of mainland Florida knows of them. They are among the first islands one encounters after leaving the mainland. There are two of them: Upper Matecumbe Key and Lower Matecumbe Key.

That's where Mel began his search, using a fast boat named the *Buccaneer*. Working from daybreak until nightfall, Mel and his crew seldom took a day off. At night, he would tie up the boat to his pier and give the crew a list of repairs that had to be made. When he returned to the pier at dawn the next morning, the boat was ready to go.

Weeks went by. Several times the magnetometer and mailboxes together uncovered sunken ships. But none was the *Atocha*. Mel would mark each site with a buoy. Then he would sign up another salvage company to work the wreck, with Treasure Salvors to receive a share of anything recovered. Mel himself was not interested in rummaging through just any wreck. He wanted the *Atocha*.

Mel interrupted searching only long enough to fly to Spain to visit the archives in the hope of finding a map or document that would tell him exactly where the *Atocha* went down. He made two trips to Spain; both ended in failure.

The first time Mel looked at the documents available at the Archives of the Indies in Seville, his heart sank. They were meaningless to him. He could not make out a single word. While the language in which the documents were written was somewhat similar to modern-day Spanish, the problem was with the handwriting. Each document was written in a flowing script of rounded letters that bore not the slightest resemblance to the way written characters look today. Mel didn't speak much Spanish, but even if he had, it would have made no difference. The document script was mere gibberish to him.

To make things even worse, there was no punctuation: no commas, no periods—nothing. The script appeared as one endless sentence, stretching through thousands of pages. As if this was not bad enough, the ink had faded on some documents until it was not much darker than the paper itself.

The great number of documents was yet another problem. They were tied together into bundles that were eight to ten inches thick. Each of the thousands of bundles contained many hundreds of documents in no particular order. One was often completely unrelated to the one next to it.

Mel saw that trying to make any sense out of the documents was an impossible task. He hired Ángeles Flores Rodríguez, an expert in document research, to help him. He explained what he was looking for: some clue as to where the *Atocha* and other ships in the 1622 Mainland Fleet had gone down.

After his return to Florida, Mel heard from Señora Rodríguez

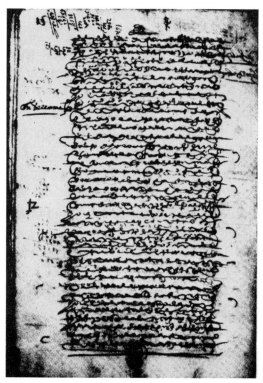

Documents in the Archives of the Indies, written in flowing script, were almost impossible to translate. (R. Duncan Mathewson)

from time to time. Her answers were always the same: The *Atocha* had sunk somewhere off "the Keys of Matecumbe." Mel could only shake his head in frustration. By now he had searched every square inch of an area that included the Matecumbe Keys and stretched north as far as Key Largo. He had not found even a sign of the *Atocha*.

Fisher then moved his base of operations farther down the Keys to Marathon. From there, they searched the lower-central Keys. Again, nothing. Months had now passed. There had to be another answer.

Help came from an unexpected source. Several years before, when the Fishers had been living in Vero Beach, Mel and Deo had met tall, studious Eugene Lyon, a teacher at a local community college, and his wife. Lyon, a scholar, impressed the Fishers with the ease with which he could translate Mel's Spanish treasure books into English. To Lyon, Mel was a romantic figure, an adventurer. The families became close friends.

In 1967, Lyon returned to college to study for an advanced degree in Latin American history. This involved reading old Spanish documents. His research eventually took him to the Archives of the Indies in Seville.

When Mel learned that Lyon was going to Spain to work in the archives, he asked him to look for documents that mentioned the *Atocha*. It didn't take Lyon long to find such documents. One group of them seemed very important. They dated to 1626 and were titled "Accounts of Francisco Núñez Melián." It was Melián who, with his diving bell, had been successful in salvaging gold and silver from the *Santa Margarita*, after having failed in his efforts to find the *Atocha*. Lyon turned the pages slowly. Many were pocked with wormholes, which made the strange-looking script even more difficult to read.

Eugene Lyon (left), shown here with Mel Fisher, helped to solve the mystery as to where the *Atocha* was to be found. (Pat Clyne)

Melián had worked at the *Santa Margarita* site for more than four years. Lyon was aware of Melián's contract with Philip IV. The contract stated that the king would receive one-third of any recovered treasure, one-third would go to Melián, and one-third would go toward paying Melián's expenses.

Since he was going to be repaid for whatever he spent, Melián made a careful record of all his purchases. Every coil of rope, every barrel of water, and every pulley wheel was listed, along with the cost of each. The tabulation filled page after page. Lyon estimated there were several hundred of them.

Reading the pages was not easy, even for someone as fluent in Spanish as Lyon was. But he bore on, fascinated by the documents and their rich detail. He felt almost as if he were being transported back to the seventeenth century.

Lyon frequently came upon the phrase *Cayos de Matecumbe*, "the Keys of Matecumbe." These references seemed to confirm what other documents had stated: the *Atocha* and *Santa Margarita* had gone down in the vicinity of the Matecumbe Keys.

But another name kept appearing in the documents: *Cayos del Marqués*. Melián, Lyon read, had found the wreck of the *Santa Margarita* in the Keys of the Marquis. In one two-hour stretch of reading, Lyon encountered the term five times.

That night Lyon puzzled over the two terms. Most of the documents concerning the 1622 Mainland Fleet said that the ships had gone down in the Keys of Matecumbe. Now something new had been added—Keys of the Marquis.

What did it mean?

Lyon began studying old books and maps to find out more about the two names. He soon learned that Matecumbe had once been a general name, one that the Spanish used for all the islands that now make up the Florida Keys.

Through the years, individual names came to be applied to each of the islands. Only two of them, Upper Matecumbe Key and Lower Matecumbe Key, still carried the original name. That meant it didn't make sense for modern-day treasure seekers to look for the *Atocha, Santa Margarita,* or other ships of the 1622 Mainland Fleet near those islands only.

Several old maps that Lyon consulted used the name Cayos del Marqués in referring to the group of islands lying about twenty-five miles west of the present day Key West. On modern maps, these islands are known as the Marquesas Keys.

That was it! That was where the *Atocha* could be found— near the Marquesas Keys.

Although Lyon had uncovered a vital clue concerning the whereabouts of the sunken ships, he continued to be puzzled. Lyon was aware that Fisher, Art McKee, Burt Webber, and other treasure hunters had consulted documents in the Archives of the Indies. Why, Lyon wanted to know, were they unable to discover that the *Atocha* and other ships of the Mainland Fleet went down off the Marquesas Keys? Lyon eventually figured that out, too. Fisher and the rest had worked with documents that dated to the year 1622, the year the *Atocha* and the other ships sank. In 1622, the Cayos del Marqués, the Marquesas Keys of the present day, were nameless. It was Lyon who learned that the islands were named in 1623 by Gaspar de Vargas to honor the Marquis de Cadereita, who had assigned Vargas to salvage the sunken galleons of the Mainland Fleet.

It was several years before the name Cayos del Marqués began to appear on maps and other documents. The searchers had simply gone back to documents that were too early.

Lyon wrote to Fisher and told him what he had discovered: that both the *Atocha* and *Santa Margarita* were resting in waters off the Marquesas Keys. That put them at least a hundred miles to the south and west of Upper and Lower Matecumbe Keys.

Not long after, Fisher moved his base of operations to Key West, close to Marquesas Keys. By the summer of 1970, he was ready to begin again.

Heading south in the United States, you can't go any farther than Key West. (George Sullivan)

8 ⤺

A Teasing Trail

K ey West, the last major island of the Florida Keys, is the southernmost city in the continental United States. About 25,000 people call it home. It is not big, about four miles long and a mile wide. Havana, Cuba, is only ninety miles away, directly south.

Key West is "easy livin'." Tourism is one of the two major industries. (Commercial fishing is the other.) Tourists stroll the streets of Old Town, bathed in tropical breezes and thumping music from open-air saloons.

Ernest Hemingway, a widely hailed short-story writer and novelist, and winner of the Nobel Prize for Literature in 1954, lived in Key West for many years. "I like Key West," he once said, "because the people don't stare at me."

Key West is like that. No one much cares who you are or what you do. The rules of conduct are softened a bit.

When it comes to treasure salvage, Key West has a long, rich history. In fact, beginning in the 1820s and continuing for the next forty years or so, Key West was the wrecking capital of the world. Just about the entire population was involved in salvaging the cargoes of vessels that smashed into the coral reefs off the island.

Salvaged anchors and similar objects dot the Key West landscape. (George Sullivan)

Wrecking was big business. During a ten-year period beginning in 1848, a total of 499 wrecked ships were recorded, an average of almost one a week.

An admiralty court was established to regulate the industry. The captain of each wrecking vessel was licensed by the court. A license was not granted unless the applicant could prove he was an honest man with no criminal record.

When a wreck was sighted, the wreckers raced to the reef in their boats. The first boat to reach the damaged vessel and get the captain's permission to go aboard became the master of the wrecking operation. Before removing the cargo, however, the master first had to see to it that the passengers and crew were safe.

Key West museum pays homage to the wrecking profession. (George Sullivan)

The laws governing the industry required that all cargo recovered be brought to Key West for auction. Buyers came from Charleston, South Carolina; Mobile, Alabama; New Orleans, New York, and Havana. They bid on drugs and medicines, boots and shoes, books and furniture, laces and linens, casks of wine and barrels of china.

Today, some historians estimate that more than four thousand wrecks lie in the waters just off the Florida Keys. Tennessee Reef is where the navy battleship U.S.S. *Tennessee* went aground in the 1930s. There's the "pot wreck" off the Middle Keys, where a boat laden with bales of marijuana was scuttled by its crew when halted for illegal drug trafficking. At Rock Key off Key West, amateur divers search for remnants of a Spanish sailing ship that dates to the late 1700s.

As this suggests, storms and hurricanes are an important part of Key West history. (A tropical storm becomes a hurricane when its winds reach a velocity greater than seventy-three miles an hour.) A hurricane in 1910 picked up a Key West house and turned it completely around—its back door now faces the street.

Thanks to modern-day forecasting methods, Key West residents now get several days of warning before a hurricane strikes. Nevertheless, hurricanes still cause widespread damage, and they claim the lives of residents—as Hurricane Donna did in 1966.

Mel Fisher established his headquarters in Key West in 1970. With his relaxed and rather casual manner, he quickly blended into the local scene. In time, however, he himself and the treasure he eventually recovered were to become one of the island's chief attractions.

When Fisher arrived in Key West, all he knew from what Lyon had told him was that the *Atocha* had gone down somewhere in the waters surrounding the Marquesas Keys, an area more than thirty miles long and five miles wide. In other words, Lyon had merely put Fisher in the ballpark. Now he had to find the right seat.

Fisher began to hire divers, mostly boys in their twenties. They had read of Fisher and what he was planning to do and had ventured to Key West from every part of the country. Fisher paid them $2.75 an hour. They were given their food and a place to sleep aboard the salvage boat, often a mattress on an open deck. No one complained. After all, it was the chance to participate in the adventure of a lifetime.

The magnetometer was the basic tool Fisher used. For the magnetometer to register a hit, it had to be brought within fifty or so feet of an iron deposit: an iron anchor, a cannon, cannonballs, spikes or nails.

The boat dragged the magnetometer back and forth over a carefully charted rectangle of the ocean's surface. The method used was similar to the way in which a farmer seated on a tractor plows a field. Each line had to be perfectly straight and exactly the same distance from the line on either side of it. If the lines were too close together, the boat captain was duplicating effort, searching an area that had already been searched. If the lines were too far apart, he was missing areas.

Controlling the search pattern was not difficult as long as the boat was in sight of the coastline. The boat captain then designated the land as one side of the rectangle. Tall stakes, painted in Day-Glo colors, were driven into the beach at intervals of fifty feet. The boat captain would run his search pattern by making reference to the stakes, first steering the boat straight toward the beach, turning, and then running straight toward the open ocean. He'd drop a buoy at the end of each run, then start a new one.

This was the technique that Fisher's boats used when searching off the Upper and Lower Matecumbes. But when he began working off the Marquesas, he often moved out into open ocean. The islands were then reduced to low, green spots on the horizon, too far away to be useful.

How would Fisher control the search pattern?

He decided he would rely on a theodolite. Used in surveying, the theodolite is a precision instrument with a telescopic sight that enables the user to establish accurate angles and distances.

Fisher used bolts and long strips of angle iron to build tall towers on the ocean floor. Atop each he mounted a platform for a theodolite. The idea was for the theodolite operator to track the boat as it pulled the magnetometer through the water, radioing the captain whenever his course needed correction.

Working as a theodolite operator could be brutal. Early in the morning, the operator would be brought to the tower. All he had with him were his instruments, a CB radio, his lunch, a plastic milk bottle filled with water, and some toilet paper. He would spend the first hour or so leveling his tripod and setting the instrument. Once that had been done, he would stand for hours with his eye to the eyepiece, holding the boat in the crosshairs. If he moved the instrument even a fraction of an inch, it had to be reset, which took valuable time.

All day long the operator stood on his cramped perch. The hot tropical sun baked him, and there was no relief from it. Divers called the theodolite operators "fry boys."

Fisher held out a reward for those involved in this exhausting work. In the morning, before the magnetometer search began, the fry boys were allowed to dive on some of the hits that had been recorded the day before. Then it was back to the tower.

There was never any shortage of hits. But the finds that resulted were mostly iron junk. Fisher and his divers found metal fish traps and big oil drums. They found World War II torpedoes, explosive mines, and bombs used in practice runs

Theodolite towers helped in guiding the use of the magnetometer. (Pat Clyne)

by navy aircraft. They found a wrecked airplane and an old paddlewheel steamer.

Fisher himself dove down one day and after the mailboxes had dug a crater, he found meteorites, masses of stone and metal that fall to the earth from outer space. They registered on the magnetometer chart just as any other big chunk of iron would.

Week after week passed without any sign of the *Atocha*. Fisher tried to figure it out. He thought it might be the fault of the fry boys. Maybe through carelessness or lack of experience they had given the boat captains faulty instructions. As a result, maybe wide strips of the ocean had never been covered. Or maybe their lack of success was caused by the magnetometer itself. Sometimes one of the instrument's wires worked loose and the mag went dead. Maybe a nonfunctioning magnetometer had passed right over the *Atocha*.

Fisher and his boats worked throughout the fall and winter. When spring came again they were still at it. A project that Fisher thought might take two or three months had already used up an entire year. Fisher's costs were sometimes running as high as a thousand dollars a day, and he had nothing to show for his efforts.

Early in 1971, Mel's luck changed. He had surveyed an area that was located about ten miles west of the Marquesas, and had marked the "mag" hits with buoys. Fisher himself went down as the mailboxes blasted away. With the sand swirling about in the green water, Fisher suddenly spotted a metal hoop the size of a bicycle tire. He knew immediately what it was: a barrel hoop. There had been a great number of storage barrels aboard the *Atocha*, Mel knew. Iron hoops held the wooden staves together.

Encrusted barrel hoop marked the trail to the *Atocha* and its treasure. (George Sullivan)

Then Fisher found a musket ball, a solid ball of lead about the size of a child's marble. Soldiers aboard the *Atocha* were armed with handguns that fired musket balls.

Back on board, Fisher was jubilant. "This is it!" he cried. "We've found the *Atocha*!"

There was no way of knowing that, of course. The best that could be said was that perhaps the musket balls had once belonged to soldiers who served aboard the *Atocha*. Perhaps. They could easily have come from some other ship.

Not long after the musket balls had been found, divers recovered a huge anchor. Its shank was sixteen feet long. At the end of the shank was a ring so big that a man could swim through it. It was the kind of anchor that had once been carried aboard Spanish galleons.

The best was yet to come. Don Kincaid, a twenty-five-year-old photographer who wanted experience in taking pictures underwater, had joined Mel's team. There was little to photograph in the area where the divers were working, however. The sea bottom was smooth sand, offering little of interest. And when the dive boat *Virgalona* switched on its mailboxes, churning up the sand, Kincaid's cameras were made virtually useless.

One day, Kincaid was diving in clear water in a big crater that had been hollowed out by the *Virgalona*'s mailboxes. Something bright caught his eye. He swam over to it. It was a chain, several feet long. To Kincaid it looked like brass. He wasn't impressed by it, thinking that maybe one of the divers had tossed the chain into the crater to fool him. There was another diver in the hole with him. He held the chain up for the other man to see. The diver shrugged; he didn't seem to think much of it either.

Kincaid decided he would show his find to Mel and the crew of the *Virgalona*, even though it meant he might be laughed at.

Don Kincaid found the first of the *Atocha*'s gold. (Pat Clyne)

As he got closer to the surface and the light of day made everything brighter, the chain, as Kincaid was to say later, started getting "golder and golder." When he broke the surface, he held the chain above his head. A diver aboard the *Virgalona* saw it and let out a scream. Once Kincaid was on board, other divers shook his hand and clapped him on the back. Deo Fisher hugged him. Mel started to cry.

The chain was gold. It was eight-and-a-half feet long. Each of its links was three-eighths of an inch in length. Fisher said the chain was worth $120,000, but that was just a guess. Fisher rewarded Kincaid by giving him a gold coin.

Kincaid's gold chain was the first of many that Fisher and his divers were to find. Archaeologists and historians marvel at them. They range in length from a few inches to twelve feet. One weighed six-and-a-half pounds. Historians believe that the chains were the personal property of wealthy passengers. The links of some chains are exactly the same weight as the gold escudo coin of the period. When a chain owner wanted to buy something, he or she would simply twist off a link, just as someone today puts forth cash or a credit card to make a purchase.

Gold chains were worn by both sexes. Worn by women, they encircled the neck. Sometimes they were studded with emeralds, pearls, or other gems. Worn by men, they hung about the shoulders.

With the finding of Kincaid's chain, gold fever swept the *Virgalona*. Other boats arrived on the scene. Their crew members clambered aboard the *Virgalona* to look at the chain, handle it, and drape it around their shoulders.

As the first piece of treasure from the Spanish shipwreck of 1622, Kincaid's gold chain had special significance. But an even more important find was made later that year. A diver unearthed a blackened, irregular-shaped clump of metal. Fisher immediately recognized it as a cluster of silver coins. A diver broke the clump into pieces. It contained nineteen silver coins. Several had *P* mint marks, indicating that they had come from the huge Potosí mine and mint, which at the time was part of Peru. One of the coins was dated 1619, and none had dates later than 1622.

The coins seemed to have come from the 1622 fleet. But if they did, which ship were they from: the *Atocha*, the *Santa Margarita*, or some other, unknown vessel? No one could answer the question.

Months went by before anything else of importance was found. Mel's search had already cost him more than he had ever expected to spend. While it was true that he was paying his divers only $2.75 an hour, he paid them for a ten-hour day and they were usually at sea for ten days at a time. A ten-man diving crew cost him $2,750 in wages every ten days, plus the groceries they consumed.

His payroll represented only one part of his expenses. He needed a never-ending supply of masks, flippers, wet suits, tanks, and regulators—the tools of the diving trade.

Fuel was an enormous expense. Even when a boat was anchored over a site, its engines were needed to pump seawater through the mailboxes. Other engines powered pumps, compressors, and generators. Engine parts had to be replaced constantly.

Mel's need for money was like a bad toothache that wouldn't go away. He found himself spending more and more time on the telephone and in meetings, attempting to attract individuals to invest in the search.

By this time, Mel was beginning to realize that his original concept of the search had little meaning. He had started out looking for a sunken ship, a Spanish galleon with a stern and a bow, decks and masts, and anchors and cannons. But there was no ship. What they were finding was bits and pieces—some barrel hoops, clumps of coins, a few musket balls, an anchor. That was what was left of the *Atocha*. And those bits and pieces were scattered over a vast area of the ocean floor. "We were always on a trail," Mel's wife once said, "a little bit here, a little bit there. It was kind of a tease."

9

The Trail Gets Hot

W hen winter turned to spring in 1973 and the Gulf waters were calm again, Fisher renewed his search for the riches of the *Atocha*. He now had better equipment than ever. He had raised money by selling shares of stock in Treasure Salvors. He had also brought in approximately one hundred "partners" to provide financial support for the search. Some investors put up hundreds of thousands of dollars. Others contributed much smaller amounts, $1,000 or so.

The money that he obtained from investors went toward the purchase of two powerful Mississippi River tugboats, which he converted for use as salvage boats. One he named the *Northwind*, the other the *Southwind*. On each he installed mailboxes that would dig much bigger craters than any of his other boats, and dig them deeper, too.

He appointed his eldest son, Dirk, now nineteen, to be captain of the *Northwind*. He put his son Kim, seventeen, in charge of the *Southwind*. The two boats joined the *Virgalona* off the Marquesas.

In May that year, divers from the *Southwind* and *Virgalona* began following a trail of artifacts that led in a southeasterly direction from the galleon anchor that had been found two years before. They recovered muskets, swords, an iron cannonball, and dozens of silver coins.

They also found cannonballs made of stone and the remains of tightly compressed bales of indigo dyestuffs. One day the *Virgalona*'s twin mailboxes happened to send a prop blast toward the bales of indigo, which appeared as big clumps of blue clay, and as a result a patch of sea water turned blue. When the divers came to the surface, their faces and bodies were stained with seventeenth-century dye.

During the last week of May, after the *Virgalona*'s mailboxes had hollowed out a crater, divers went down to find that the sides of the hole were studded with lumpy masses of blackened metal. They had struck a pocket of silver coins. All of the divers were sent into the water. When they fanned the sides of the crater with their hands to move the sand, more black blobs

Found at the *Atocha* site, these Spanish pieces of eight were all minted in Mexico. (Treasure Salvors)

were revealed. One diver returned to the surface, dumped the coins he had gathered on the *Virgalona*'s deck, and said, "I've been to the bank." From that time on, the crater was known as the Bank of Spain. On the first day the "bank" was open, divers "withdrew" 1,460 silver coins.

Fisher believed that he had found the remains of a treasure chest. He was walking on air as a result of the finds, not only because of what he had found but because he thought he was close to the *Atocha*'s strongroom. If he was, there were seventy-five other treasure chests down there.

Sometimes there were as many as six or seven divers working the area at once. They would swim along the sides of the crater, scooping up the blackened lumps of coins and dropping them into mesh bags. They called them goodie bags. At first it was fun to fill the bags and dump their contents onto the deck and hear the "oohs" and "aahs" from the crew as they gathered round. But eventually the divers grew tired. It was hard work. Instead of hauling the bags to the surface, the divers made a pile of them at the bottom of the crater. They were then loaded into plastic milk crates and hoisted aboard the salvage boat by means of a winch.

The *Virgalona*'s mailboxes eventually blew away the sand all the way to the bedrock. There were even more coins stuck to the rock itself. Divers popped these free with screwdrivers.

Some six thousand silver coins were recovered from the Bank of Spain. According to the mint marks they bore, most of them had been coined at Potosí, Mexico City, and Lima. But no one could tell what vessel they had come from.

Dirk Fisher made an amazing find that summer. After scanning a shallow crater dug by the *Northwind*'s mailboxes, Dirk surfaced near the stern of the boat with a heavy circle of bronze in one hand. In the weeks that followed, the importance of the object was revealed.

For seventeenth-century mariners, the astrolabe was a vital piece of navigational equipment. (George Sullivan)

Dirk had found an astrolabe, the principal navigation instrument for ships of the *Atocha*'s day. The numbers indicating degrees could be easily read on the instrument's circular face, and its pointer still swung freely like a compass needle.

The astrolabe was used by Spanish mariners for figuring a ship's latitude. Later research identified the astrolabe as having come from the workshop of Lope Homen, a Portuguese instrument maker who worked from 1517 to 1567.

Fisher said the astrolabe might be worth $300,000. But it was as a historical artifact that the object was valued. "It was," wrote Eugene Lyon in his book, *The Search for the Atocha*, "with the mariner's compass, a basic tool of European man's courageous expansion into hitherto unknown seas while seeking a new world."

After almost three years of hard work in waters off the Marquesas, Fisher and his divers were at least making important finds. But they were still not sure what ship the valuables were coming from. Were they from the *Atocha*? The *Santa Margarita*? Or some other vessel? No one could say.

The Fourth of July was no holiday aboard the *Southwind*. The divers were in the waters not long after daybreak. Kane Fisher, Mel's youngest son, now fourteen, was one of them.

Late in the morning, Kane and another diver entered the water near the *Southwind*'s stern. As they headed for the bottom, they peered downward, hoping to spy something valuable. Suddenly Kane saw an unusual shape. It was oblong, with a smooth and blackened surface, shaped something like a shoebox. Later, Kane would say it "looked like a loaf of bread."

Kane tugged at the object, but it was so heavy he could not move it. He hurried to the surface and called out to crewmen aboard the *Southwind*, "I think I've found a bar of silver." Other divers went down with ropes to help him bring it up.

As the crew was examining the bar on the *Southwind*'s open deck, another diver found a second bar. Then a third was found.

News of the extraordinary find was radioed to Treasure Salvors's office in Key West. Fisher grabbed a speedboat and was aboard the *Southwind* by midafternoon.

The three silver bars rested in an open fiberglass tank filled

Diver displays a silver bar from the *Atocha*, one of the many hundreds eventually recovered. (George Sullivan)

with sea water. Through the water, onlookers could see that the upper surface of each bar was inscribed with numbers and symbols. "Call Gene Lyon," Fisher cried when he heard the bars were so marked. "Tell him we've got some silver bars for him to identify." Fisher knew that Lyon had copies of the cargo lists from both the *Atocha* and *Santa Margarita*. Perhaps the numbers and symbols on the bars could be matched with information on one of the cargo lists.

When Lyon arrived by speedboat, there were about forty people aboard the *Southwind*. A celebration was under way. Fisher led Lyon to the deck where the ingots lay in the fiberglass tank. He asked that they be removed so that he could examine them more closely. Each bore a number in Roman numerals. The three bars Fisher's divers had found were numbered 569, 794, 4584. They also had markings that Lyon knew referred to the purity of the silver, and there were shipping marks. Lyon copied the information from each bar, then returned to Key West.

The next morning when the public library opened its doors, Lyon was there. He brought with him microfilm reels that contained the cargo lists of the *Atocha* and *Santa Margarita*. The first reel he threaded into the viewer represented the *Santa Margarita*. The bars, Lyon had been told, had been recovered in twenty-five feet of water. That was the depth of the water in which the *Santa Margarita* had sunk. The *Atocha* went down in fifty-five feet of water.

There were 411 silver bars listed for the *Santa Margarita*. Lyon checked through the numbers one by one. Each entry was written in ancient script. It was slow going. Lyon worked all day without finding a number that matched those on the bars.

Lyon was back at the library the next day, poring over the microfilm. He worked that day, the next day, and the day after that. None of the bars was registered on the *Santa Margarita*'s cargo list. Lyon then turned to the manifest for the *Atocha*. It was twice the length of the *Santa Margarita*'s list, bearing the identification numbers for 901 bars. Lyon first checked the numbers for the bars that were loaded aboard the *Atocha* in

Havana. No luck. Then he began searching the list of bars that had been loaded in Cartagena. Suddenly his heart skipped a beat. There it was—4584, the identification number of one of the bars that had been found by the *Southwind*'s diver.

According to the manifest, the bar had been shipped in payment of the Crown license on black slaves who had been sold in Cartagena. Its weight was given as a little more than 63½ pounds. Later, Lyon identified the other two bars, 569 and 764, as coming from the *Atocha*.

When the *Southwind* entered Key West harbor and eased up to the Treasure Salvors's pier, a joyous crowd was on hand. A freight scale had been ordered and was waiting. It had been preset at 63.6 pounds, the exact weight of bar 4584. The bar was to be placed upon the scale. If the bar weighed 63.6 pounds, it would be the final proof Lyon wanted.

The silver bar bearing number 4584 was carried from the *Southwind* and placed on the scale. The crowd pressed forward. Photographers and television camera crews recorded the scene. Fisher stared at the scale. The bar weighed 63.6 pounds exactly. Fisher proclaimed, "We have found the *Atocha*."

Fisher was wrong again. In truth, his search for the golden galleon was not much beyond the starting point. Years of hard work and anguish were to follow.

During the summer of 1973, Fisher became involved in several hot disputes with officials representing the state of Florida. They charged that he was not filling out all the reports he was supposed to submit, that he was not keeping accurate maps of the sites that he had dug, and that he wasn't giving the proper treatment to artifacts he had recovered. They were not being carefully cataloged and little effort was being made to preserve them. State officials were so upset by Mel's failings that they threatened to withdraw his salvage contract.

Bleth McHaley, the director of public relations for Treasure Salvors, thought she had a way to calm the officials. She advised Mel to hire a professional archaeologist, someone who could be handed the responsibility of conducting a scientific study of the sites and the artifacts recovered from them.

Mel made a good choice. He hired R. Duncan Mathewson.

R. Duncan Mathewson joined Treasure Salvors as head archaeologist in 1973. (George Sullivan)

Tall and energetic, with tousled hair, chin whiskers, and a raspy voice, Mathewson had once served as an archaeologist for the government of the island of Jamaica. There he had gained experience in excavating sixteenth- and seventeenth-century Spanish sites. He had also done archaeological work in West Africa.

Mathewson had a growing fascination for shipwreck archaeology. "Unlike sites on land," he once said, "a shipwreck is an almost perfect snapshot of a moment in history. Cities change over the years, buildings are put up and torn down, and the character of an area's population changes. However, at the instant a ship goes down, it becomes a time capsule, entombing the people on board and the tools and possessions that exemplify their way of life." He looked upon the *Atocha* and *Santa Margarita* as "the main characters in a first-rate mystery story."

The eager and enthusiastic Mathewson immediately set to work establishing an improved cataloging system. Each artifact was given a coded number that referred to when and where it was recovered. Mathewson brought in specialists to study the pottery and other types of material that the divers were bringing up. It was the beginning of a new era for Fisher and Treasure Salvors.

10

Into Deep Water

A rchaeologists and scuba divers are often at odds with one another. Many archaeologists look upon divers as mere souvenir hunters. They accuse divers of damaging or destroying historic wrecks in their search for relics.

Many divers, on the other hand, have little patience with archaeologists, who they feel do nothing in the actual discovery of underwater sites and add unnecessary and frustrating delays to the salvage process. Take Mel Fisher, for example. Fisher gambled millions of dollars and more than a decade of effort searching for the *Atocha* and *Santa Margarita*. The vessels would still be undiscovered were it not for him.

Duncan Mathewson stood between the two warring groups. He believed that archaeologists and divers should work together to locate and recover precious historical artifacts.

Mathewson began to train Fisher's divers to do the work of real archaeologists. He showed them how to make careful measurements and prepare detailed maps before starting work on sites. All major finds were located and marked on the appropriate site map. Mathewson thus had a very clear idea of what was being recovered, and he also knew exactly where each object had been found.

Divers were now working in an area west of the Marquesas known as the Quicksands. The term *quicksand* normally refers to a bed of loose sand so saturated with water that anyone sinks who attempts to stand on it. But to Mel Fisher and his divers, the Quicksands meant an area of relatively shallow water, five to ten miles west of the Marquesas, where the ocean bottom was constantly being shifted by currents and tides.

During the summer of 1974, divers at work in the Quicksands found a few hundred coins, some ballast stones, and two small-caliber long guns, or harquebuses. They also found two gold chains, one of them nearly seven feet in length.

The divers were finding valuable treasure and artifacts; there could be no doubt about that. But Duncan Mathewson was perplexed. Big pieces of the puzzle were still missing.

Where, for instance, was the ballast pile? A galleon the size of the *Atocha* would have carried an enormous number of ballast stones within its lower hull. These were meant to lower the ship's center of gravity and help to keep it upright in the water. Where were those hundreds upon hundreds of big stones?

Mathewson also knew that a galleon such as the *Atocha* would have carried as many as five hundred olive jars, which were used for storage aboard ship. Fewer than fifty olive jars had been recovered.

As for the *Atocha*'s anchors, one had been found. But Gene Lyon, in his research in Seville, had learned that the *Atocha* had carried five main anchors, each weighing about twenty-two hundred pounds. How could the magnetometer have missed iron objects so large?

And what about the ship's bronze cannons? Twenty cannons were on board the *Atocha* when the ship sank. Not one had been discovered.

Something else nagged at Mathewson. When Gaspar de

Vargas was assigned to salvage the treasure from the *Atocha* in 1622 and found the vessel's sunken hulk, he recorded the depth of the water at fifty-four feet. Francisco Núñez Melián, who was given the contract to salvage the galleon in 1624, confirmed Vargas's findings about the water's depth. Yet Fisher's divers had found the anchor at twenty-five feet. How was one to account for the two different figures? Mathewson was bewildered.

The coins that had been recovered certainly indicated that they were on the trail of a vessel that was part of the 1622 Mainland Fleet. And the silver ingot with the number 4584 convinced Mathewson that the ship was the *Atocha*. But the quest was just beginning, Mathewson realized. "It was as if we had found the scene of the crime and had clearly identified the victim," said Mathewson. "Now, where was the corpse?"

To find the "corpse," Mathewson went back to the archaeological data he had gathered, to his charts and maps. They showed the artifacts to be scattered in a clear trail that led south and east toward deep water.

Mathewson began to theorize about what had happened to the *Atocha* after the ship sank. He knew that when Vargas had first seen the vessel it had been intact. Its mizzenmast had been sticking out of the water. When the second hurricane struck, the ship's superstructure must have been wrenched free and swept from the deep water. It struck the edge of the Quicksands, scattering light objects—coins, cannon balls, small weapons, pieces of jewelry, and shards of pottery—everywhere.

The *Atocha*'s hull and the great bulk of its rich cargo, Mathewson believed, still lay in deep water to the southeast, close to the reef that had ripped open the vessel's hull in 1622. Not everyone agreed with Mathewson. The fact that the *Atocha* had sunk in fifty-five feet of water did not mean that it still rested in water that deep. Through the centuries, the sands on the bottom of the ocean could have been rearranged over and

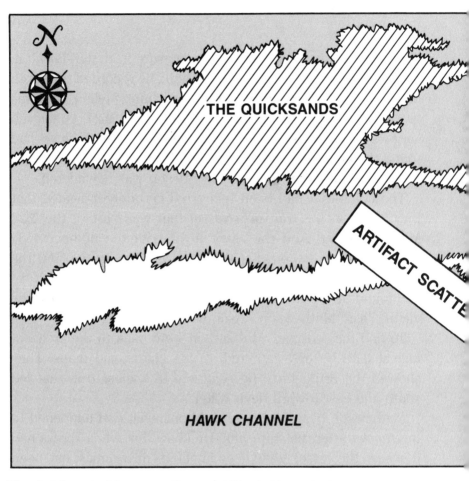

The Quicksands, Marquesas Keys, and Hawk Channel, showing the trail

over again. Or storms could have moved the vessel from its original site into water that was deeper or shallower.

And there was other evidence that Mathewson might be on the wrong track. Whenever one of Fisher's boats had probed a deep-water site, divers had found nothing. Many divers, boat captains, and other members of the Treasure Salvors staff shrugged off Mathewson's theory. They were convinced that the *Atocha* and its treasure were in the Quicksands.

As for Fisher himself, he was wary of deep water. It created hazards for the divers. Diving to thirty feet or beyond could

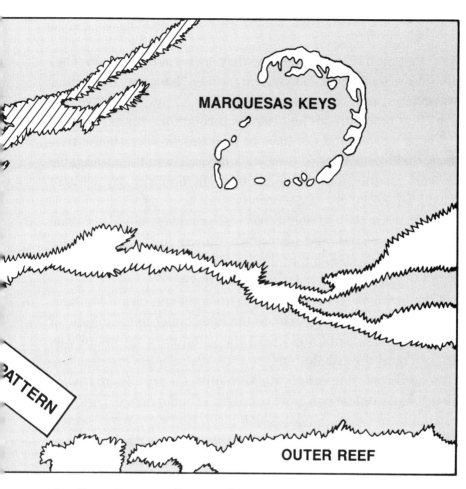

MARQUESAS KEYS

PATTERN

OUTER REEF

of artifacts that were discovered.

lead to decompression sickness, caisson disease—what divers called the bends.

When a diver descends in deep water, nitrogen is dissolved in the bloodstream and body tissues. As long as the diver keeps descending or remains at the bottom, there is no problem. But when he ascends, should he come up too fast, small bubbles of nitrogen can form, with tragic results. A diver can experience intense pain in the joints. In serious cases, the bends can cause loss of consciousness, or even death.

To avoid getting the bends, divers working at deep levels

have to limit the amount of time they spend at the bottom. They also have to ascend slowly, sometimes "hanging" in shallow water for specific amounts of time. This allows the nitrogen to leave the bloodstream and tissues through the lungs.

Fisher's divers did not have to face this problem in the relatively shallow waters of the Quicksands. There they were able to work at the bottom for up to eight hours a day without having to worry about decompression sickness.

Mathewson had no doubt that Fisher's divers could continue to find silver, gold, and historical artifacts in the Quicksands. But he was convinced that the *Atocha* itself and the main treasure pile, the mother lode, were not there.

"The artifacts were speaking to me loud and clear," Mathewson said. "They told me to go to the deep water in the middle of Hawk Channel. Until Mel heard the same message, there was little I could do to help him."

Gene Lyon supported Mathewson's theory. So did Dirk Fisher, Mel's oldest son, now twenty-one and married. Dirk was captain of the salvage boat *Northwind*. His wife, Angel, served as a member of the *Northwind*'s crew. She kept the log, photographed artifacts the divers recovered, and often did the cooking.

Dirk had recently completed schooling in commercial deep-sea diving. That, thought Duncan Mathewson, may have contributed to his enthusiasm for the deep-water theory.

In the summer of 1975, Dirk headed the *Northwind* south and east of the Quicksands toward Hawk Channel and into an area the divers called "Mud Deep." Here the bedrock dipped sharply and the water reached forty feet in depth. The bottom was hard-packed clay and limestone over rock.

On a Sunday morning in July, with the *Northwind* at anchor, Dirk dove into the water and swam deep. The day before, there had been a problem with the anchors, which kept slipping. Dirk had gone down to take a look. He was about a hundred feet off of the *Northwind*'s bow, gliding swiftly through the murky gray-green water, when he came upon a bulky mass of long, heavy, greenish objects. They were cannons, bronze cannons, a rare prize.

Dirk sped to the surface. When his head came out of the water, he started screaming at the top of his lungs in the direction of the *Northwind*: "We're rich! We're rich! Get a buoy!"

While crew members hurried to get a buoy to mark the spot, Dirk hurried down for another look. Bronze cannons, Dirk knew, were rarer than gold. His father had been looking for bronze cannons all of his life and never found one. Now Dirk had discovered five of them. He touched them one by one, then swam to the surface again. "Bronze cannons!" he shouted. "Five bronze cannons!"

Dirk also found some ballast stones and a copper ingot near the cannons. He was sure that he had found the *Atocha* itself. Each of those cannons weighed a ton or more. How could an object that heavy have traveled any great distance from where the ship itself sank? All he had to do, thought Dirk, was blast the area with the *Northwind*'s mailboxes a few times, and the galleon would be revealed for all to see.

Dirk agreed to hold off long enough to allow Duncan Mathewson to map and photograph the site. Mathewson rushed out to the *Northwind* the next day, and directed operations as the mailboxes blew loose sand off the sea bed. Dirk paced the deck, anxious to begin the hunt for the gold and silver.

Other divers went down to look at the cannons. One of them found a cannonball. Another discovered three tiny pieces of gold; they looked like beads. When Pat Clyne went down after the mailboxes had dug briefly, he spotted two more cannons. After more digging, still another pair was found. That made nine cannons in all.

Bronze cannon found by Dirk Fisher is hoisted from the sea bottom. (Pat Clyne)

By the end of the week, Mathewson had completed mapping and photographing the site. Two of the cannons were then hoisted aboard the *Northwind,* an operation that took an entire day. Both were eight feet long, green with age, and slightly encrusted with coral. One bore numbers, including the year it was made: 1607. It had a coat of arms and sculpted images of two dolphins on the barrel. Also stamped there was the number 3110, which Mathewson knew stood for 3,110 pounds, the cannon's weight.

Mathewson got out a list of the *Atocha*'s cannons, which Gene Lyon had sent to him from Seville. As he scanned the list and his eyes saw the number 3110, Mathewson's face broke into a wide grin. "Here it is!" he shouted. "This cannon comes from the *Atocha*."

Mel Fisher, who had arrived at the scene by this time, announced that the cannons were worth about twenty thousand dollars apiece. But to Duncan Mathewson, their value could not be measured in terms of dollars and cents. They were a critical link that connected the artifacts scattered in the Quicksands with the *Atocha*'s hull, which he believed rested seven or eight miles to the south and east in the deep water of Hawk Channel.

Most people aboard the *Northwind* shrugged off Mathewson's theory, believing that the cannons were proof that the *Atocha* was nearby. In another day of digging, maybe another week, they would find it. Everyone was confident and happy.

Sunday, July 19, was Angel Fisher's birthday. There was a quiet party for her aboard the *Northwind*, anchored off the Marquesas. The *Virgalona* was nearby, anchored about four miles away. They were barely visible to one another.

At the party, one of the divers, Rick Gage, gave Angel a necklace he had made out of shells he had found. Another gave her a painting of a sunset. Angel, Dirk, and the crew discussed the next day's diving. When they retired, there was hardly a breeze and the sea was calm.

Early the next morning, crewmen aboard the *Virgalona* awakened to a puzzling sight. The *Northwind* was nowhere to be seen. There was rivalry between the crews as to which one might be the first to find the *Atocha*'s sunken hull. Someone said the big tug might have left early in an effort to get a jump on the *Virgalona*.

The *Virgalona* hoisted anchor and headed south and west, toward the spot where the cannons had been found. Suddenly one of the crew members saw a flash of color in the water. Drawing closer, the *Virgalona*'s crew could see it was a seat cushion with seven men clinging to it. A young boy was kneeling on the cushion and waving a flashlight. The boy was Keith

Curry, Angel Fisher's twelve-year-old brother. Keith had been aboard the *Northwind*.

As the *Virgalona* pulled close to the makeshift raft, Don Kincaid, one of the men clinging to it, said, "The *Northwind* sank." Once aboard the *Virgalona*, Kincaid radioed the Coast Guard to tell them of the sinking. He also passed along the tragic news that Angel, Dirk, and Gage were thought to have drowned.

When divers from the *Virgalona* found the sunken *Northwind*, they confirmed that sad fact: all three crew members were dead.

Later, Don Kincaid explained what had happened. Before dawn on Sunday morning, he had awakened with the strange feeling that something was wrong. He quickly realized that the *Northwind*, which was still at anchor, was leaning alarmingly to one side. Upon investigation, he and the ship's engineer found a leaking valve. Water was flooding in. Before they could repair the valve, the *Northwind* toppled over onto its side and began to go down. Angel, Dirk, and Rick Gage were trapped inside as the boat sank.

Back at the headquarters of Treasure Salvors, newspaper reporters asked Mel for a statement. "It's a powerful ocean," he said sadly. "It takes people and ships."

Mel had invested six years in his search for the *Atocha*. He had spent millions of dollars for boats and equipment and divers' salaries. And now the quest had cost the Fishers the lives of a son, a daughter-in-law, and a young diver.

11 ←

The *Santa Margarita*

The Fishers were wracked with grief by the sinking of the *Northwind* and the deaths of the three young people. Deo was especially hard hit by the tragedy. She wept often. Mel did not like to leave her side. Eventually both returned to Treasure Salvors to carry on the company's work.

In the spring of 1976, Fisher resumed the search for the *Atocha*, concentrating on the area where Dirk had found the bronze cannons. The deep water there presented new problems. Going down in forty to fifty feet of water meant that the divers could make only two dives a day for a total of not much more than two hours. Otherwise, long periods of decompression in shallow water were necessary to prevent the bends.

In addition, the sea bottom was covered with a thick layer of mud, and the mud was blanketed with a hard, claylike crust, which the mailbox blasts could not punch through. Fisher equipped the search boats with water pumps and fire hoses. A diver would ram the hose nozzle into this hardpan and turn on the pump. Then a powerful jet of water would explode a hole in it. It was hard work for the divers, and slow going.

Months went by. Nothing of importance was found. Fisher

felt he was wasting his time. He wanted to go back to the Quicksands and shallower water. He knew that once he did, he would begin to find things again.

Through 1978 and 1979, Fisher's boats combed the Quicksands. The gold and silver his divers recovered helped Fisher pay his bills and kept the boats working. The finds also boosted divers' morale. But the treasure provided no new clues as to where the *Atocha* went down.

Fisher was heavily in debt now, with hardly enough money to outfit dive boats and pay crew members. Unpaid employees were suing him. The federal government was upset that tax payments were overdue, and Mel had to now add the Internal Revenue Service to the long list of those who wanted money from him.

Winter weather in the Florida Keys is sometimes stormy, keeping search boats at their piers. But the winter of 1980 was an exception, and Mel scraped together enough money to put two boats, the *Virgalona* and the *Swordfish*, into operation.

He also hired an outsider, Robert Jordan, to lend a hand. Jordan was a treasure-hunting veteran, with some twenty years' experience as a wreck diver.

Under the terms of an agreement the two worked out, Fisher would pay the operating expenses for Jordan's boat, the *Castilian*. In return, Jordan was to turn over to Fisher ninety-eight percent of any treasure he recovered from the *Atocha* and ninety-five percent of any *Santa Margarita* treasure. These were not terms that would ever make Jordan a rich man. But they were balanced by Mel's promise that he would give Jordan fifty percent of the treasure from any other wreck he happened to find.

Jordan's boat had not been at sea very long when its magnetometer registered a series of hits. One of them turned out to be a small anchor. Another was a big copper cauldron, which

Salvage boat *Swordfish* helped in finding the remains of the *Santa Margarita*. (George Sullivan)

perhaps had been used as a cooking kettle. It measured six feet across. One could cook a whole cow in a pot that big. A cauldron so large had to come from a major ship, from a vessel of galleon size, perhaps from the *Atocha* or *Santa Margarita*.

Don Kincaid, the marine photographer who had found the first of the *Atocha*'s gold more than nine years before, went aboard the *Castilian* to help direct the search. Excitement began to build. In an area a bit to the north of where the cauldron had been found, divers came upon ballast stones that carpeted the sea floor. They found shards of pottery and pieces of indigo. Then they found a small clump of silver coins. They pried them apart. There were four of them. When they were cleaned, they turned out to be Spanish pieces of eight, all of them minted before 1622.

The next finds were more spectacular. In shallower water just to the north and west of where the first artifacts had been found, divers from Jordan's boat found three heavy gold bars.

One was eleven inches long and weighed over five pounds. Five *pounds* of gold!

But what ship was it from? The markings stamped into the surface of the bars gave no clue.

Jordan went to Fisher and told him that the gold and silver were coming from neither the *Atocha* nor *Santa Margarita,* but from a new wreck. He thus claimed fifty percent of the treasure.

Fisher said no. Mel had a hunch that what Jordan was bringing up was coming from the *Santa Margarita.* He told Jordan that he would have to be satisfied with the amount they had agreed on, five percent. But Jordan would not accept that. Eventually the dispute would wind up in court.

Jordan's boat, the *Castilian,* continued to find valuable objects: a silver bell that weighed nine pounds, more clumps of silver coins, and some silver plates. He also recovered a sword and some pieces of broken pottery.

By this time, Mel's boats, the *Virgalona* and *Swordfish,* had arrived at the search area. Mel's son Kane was the captain of the *Virgalona.* One day, Kane anchored the boat over what he felt was a likely site, put on his scuba gear, and dove into the water. Once he reached the bottom, what he saw electrified him. Six silver ingots in two neat rows rested on the bedrock. His heart pounding, Kane swam over the ingots and beyond. And then he saw the wooden ribs and heavy planking that formed a section of a Spanish galleon. The partial skeleton measured twenty-three feet in length. Kane could hardly believe his eyes. This was no collection of artifacts. He had found the remains of a ship.

But what ship was it? No one could tell.

Kane and other divers from the *Virgalona* made one trip after another to the wreck site. They first brought up the six silver bars, then other silver bars they found, a gold bar, some bowls, and a silver candlestick. One of the most remarkable finds was a block of hundreds of silver coins clumped together in the form of the wooden treasure chest that had once held them. The wood had long since disintegrated into nothingness.

The silver bars recovered by Kane and the other divers bore numbers and symbols. Fisher called Eugene Lyon to see whether he could identify them. One of the bars had the number 4718 cut into it. Lyon consulted a copy of the cargo list from the *Santa Margarita*. There he found ingot number 4718 listed. Now there could be no doubt. Fisher's divers had found the remains of the *Santa Margarita*.

According to the cargo list, bar number 4718 had been shipped by Gaspar de Rojas from Portobello. It also had other markings: an *RX* and an *S* topped by a cross. Four other silver bars recovered by the divers also matched entries on the *Santa Margarita*'s cargo list.

Late that May, Jordan's divers had an exceptional day. They brought up fifteen gold bars, part of a gold disk, plus dozens of silver coins and six silver bars. The gold alone was worth more than a quarter of a million dollars.

Jordan hauled anchor and left the wreck site. He headed not for Mel Fisher's pier in Key West, but farther up the Keys. He eventually docked at Summerland Key. Fisher, who had been granted legal title to the *Santa Margarita* wreck, did not plan to allow himself to become the victim of a hijacking. He went to the authorities and forced Jordan to give up whatever treasure he had found.

Meanwhile, Fisher's divers continued to probe the wreck site. A diver from the *Swordfish* discovered a huge cannon. It bore several numbers and was decorated with a twin dolphin emblem. Eugene Lyon identified it as the largest of the *Santa Margarita*'s cannons. It weighed two tons.

Divers raise a huge cannon found at *Santa Margarita* site. (Pat Clyne)

Divers from the *Swordfish* called another day "the day of the chains." Pat Clyne found the first of them. When he sought to free it from the sand, he found that it was tangled with a second chain. And the second chain was snarled with a third. To another diver, the pile of links looked like a "hive of golden bees." That day Clyne and the other divers brought up fifteen gold chains, one of them twelve feet long.

Dick Klaudt, a diver from the *Virgalona*, found what was perhaps the most valuable object of all. He was working the side of a sand crater as it was dug by the mailboxes. Suddenly he was struck on the forehead by what looked like a yellow Frisbee. He grabbed it before it drifted away.

What Klaudt had plucked out of the ocean was a gold plate eight inches in diameter. A master craftsman of the day had

Gold plate, eight inches in diameter, the work of a master craftsman, is one of the priceless treasures from the *Santa Margarita*. (George Sullivan)

etched a design of startling beauty into the surface of the plate and around its edge. The priceless object was probably bound for the home of a Spanish nobleman.

Another diver found a bosun's pipe, or whistle, made of solid gold. On a ship such as the *Santa Margarita*, the bosun (or boatswain) was in charge of the sails, rigging, and anchors and such. He used a high-pitched whistle that was cast in the shape of a pipe to signal or issue orders to crew members.

On deck, when the diver shook the sand and seawater from the pipe, put it to his lips, and blew, it gave off a shrill whistle, a tweet that had not been heard for more than three hundred years.

The pipe was turned over to Fisher, who liked to wear it around his neck and toot it from time to time. "The last guy who wore this," he often said, "is still down there."

While some of the objects from the *Santa Margarita* were of breathtaking monetary value, others had enormous historical significance.

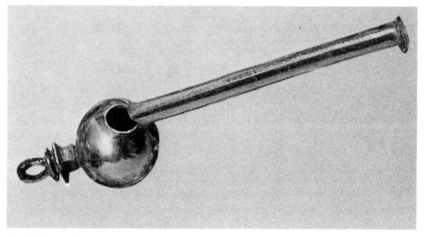

Gold bosun's pipe, although on the ocean bottom for more than three hundred years, still gave a high-pitched whistle. (George Sullivan)

With the finding of the wreckage, R. Duncan Mathewson, the head archaeologist for Treasure Salvors, initiated a careful examination of the site and the artifacts being recovered. He began by studying the ship's cargo list, which gave him a good idea of what objects and how many of each he and the divers could expect to recover. The manifest showed that the ship's cargo consisted of 419 silver bars, 118,000 silver coins, 1,488 ounces of gold in thirty-four coins and disks, copper ingots, silverware, tobacco, and indigo.

Mathewson also consulted the salvage report that had been prepared by Melián. What Melián recovered Mathewson deducted from the total.

Some of the silver bars recovered from the *Margarita* were not mentioned on the cargo list. It is believed that the people who owned these bars were attempting to smuggle them into Spain. At the time, the king was entitled to one-fifth of all silver and gold minted into coins or cast into objects of various types. By bringing the silver or gold into the country secretly, travelers might be able to avoid the king's *quinto*, or fifth, as the tax was called.

To Mathewson, the most exciting part of the wreck was the section of wooden hull. It looked like a web of wooden ribs and planking. Divers carefully removed the ballast stones from the timbers so the hull section could be measured and photographed.

When archaeologists dig a land site, one of the first things they do is divide the site into a grid. This means staking out the site into squares, with each square usually one meter by one meter. The site then resembles a sheet of graph paper. Each square in the grid is numbered. Artifacts can then be identified by the grid square in which each is recovered.

It is impossible to stake out an archaeological grid underwater. So Mathewson had a grid constructed out of red and

Grid squares made of brightly colored metal pipe enabled archaeologists to map the location of *Santa Margarita* finds. (Pat Clyne)

white plastic pipe, then lowered it into the water and laid it over the *Santa Margarita*'s hull timbers. Divers were instructed to record every artifact, no matter how tiny or insignificant it seemed to be, before moving it. In addition, each of the ship's timbers was given an identifying number and letter.

Once that work had been done, photographer Pat Clyne built a camera track above the grid. While moving the camera along the track, Clyne took a series of color photos that covered the entire site. The edges of the photos were made to overlap slightly. When they were matched together, they formed a single photographic representation of the entire site.

Mathewson was able to obtain the use of a self-propelled underwater vehicle known as the "Pegasus" to photograph the *Santa Margarita* site. The "Pegasus" looked like a torpedo. It was steered through the water by a diver. In the vehicle's nose was a special lens that automatically corrected the distortion that is normal for ordinary lenses when used underwater.

By this time, Mathewson had assigned experts to preserve and analyze the artifacts as they were brought in from the site. An archaeological laboratory began operation at Fisher's Key West headquarters. At first, Mathewson recalls, the lab was little more than a "first aid station" where artifacts were treated to stop the process of deterioration.

When iron objects come out of the water, for example, they are heavily caked with rust and corrosion. They might not even resemble their original shape. A cannonball may look like a misshapen rock, a sword blade like a loaf of French bread. Such objects have to be kept wet. If they're permitted to dry out, they can disintegrate unless they have been chemically treated. "You end up with a pile of dust," says one archaeologist. Any artifact made of wood has to be kept wet, too, until it can be treated with chemicals that act to preserve it permanently.

Gold objects need no special treatment. Salt water has little effect on them. "Gold shines forever," Mel Fisher has often said.

Some members of the archaeological team were assigned to record and catalog artifacts as they arrived. Others helped to map the hull structure. An artist with training as a ship historian created drawings of the timbers and planking as they appeared on the ocean bottom.

Just underneath the hull structure divers found pig bones and later they recovered the complete jawbone of a cow or steer, the teeth still in it. When the *Santa Margarita* sailed from Havana, the vessel apparently carried beef-on-the-hoof: The animal was to be slaughtered for food during the voyage.

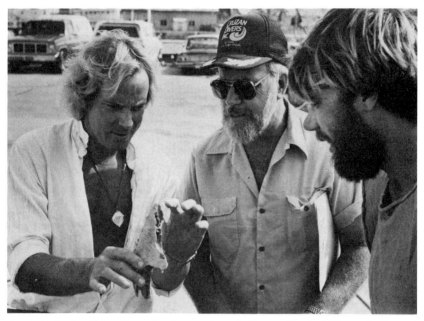

Archaeologist John Dorwin (center) and divers Curtis White (left) and Randy Barnhouse examine an animal jaw bone from the *Santa Margarita* site. (George Sullivan)

In the months that followed the initial discoveries, the *Santa Margarita* continued to yield gold chains. They eventually totaled more than 400 feet. Duncan Mathewson was puzzled. Why was so much chain aboard the ship, he wanted to know. Was it being shipped to Spain as personal jewelry by individuals who were seeking to avoid the payment of the *quinto* tax? And what was the origin of the chain? Had the links been cast in Spain or were they made in the New World by Indian goldsmiths who toiled for the Spanish?

The treasure and artifacts recovered from the *Santa Margarita* raised countless questions concerning Indian and Hispanic culture in the New World. A generation of archaeologists would be kept busy answering them.

As Fisher's divers worked the *Santa Margarita* site, it got bigger and bigger. It eventually covered a path almost a mile long. It gave up great treasure: more than 118 pounds of gold in bars and disks, 30 silver ingots, each weighing between 60 and 70 pounds, 15,000 silver coins, and 63 gold coins.

How much was the treasure worth? "The value of the gold is somewhere in the neighborhood of $12 million," Fisher told the press. At another time he said the total value of the treasure was $20 million, and still another time he mentioned $40 million. Nobody knew for sure.

Although Fisher had the treasure, whatever its value, he had no money. The state of Florida wanted a hefty share of what Fisher had found. Florida sued Fisher, carrying the case all the way to the United States Supreme Court. During the trial, Fisher was not permitted to sell what had been recovered. The treasure was kept under lock and key until the courts decided who owned what.

In 1982, Fisher's legal problems all but dissolved when the Supreme Court ruled in his favor. The treasure from the *Santa Margarita* was his, said the court, and so also would be whatever he might recover from the *Atocha*: Neither the state of Florida nor the federal government had any claim to ownership.

Fisher had been involved in courtroom squabbling for seven and a half years. Now it was all over.

At last he could devote all of his energies to the search for the *Atocha*. He had been at it for more than ten years. But his enthusiasm was not dimmed. Indeed, the *Santa Margarita* had bolstered his confidence and ambition. He was ready to move full speed ahead.

12 ←

"We Found It! We Found It!"

To be successful as a treasure hunter takes imagination and daring. It requires a questioning mind, a sense of adventure, and willingness to work hard.

And there is one other important quality: patience. Wreckers have to be able to put up with delays and misfortune. They can't let things get them down; they have to persist.

Mel Fisher had these qualities. So did his son Kane.

Like his eldest brother, Dirk, who had died when the *Northwind* sank in 1975, Kane believed that the *Atocha* and its treasure would be found in deep water, not in the Quicksands. Through the early 1980s, Kane, captain of the salvage boat *Dauntless*, doggedly pursued the theory, following a trail of artifacts that led him into Hawk Channel.

He would anchor over the hit, blast away with the mailboxes, then send divers down. Kane himself often dove with them. Most times they would find nothing. But occasionally there would be a musket ball, a spike, or a barrel hoop. "When the ship broke up, the barrels went tumbling along the bottom," Fay Feild once explained. "The hoops were still there."

When he dug a long string of empty holes, Kane would sometimes get discouraged, give up, and take the *Dauntless* back to the Quicksands. There he would make scattered finds of silver, gold, and jewelry. But he would always return to Hawk Channel and what eventually came to be known as "Kane's line."

Kane and the other boat captains were now being aided by several advances in electronic search equipment. Fay Feild, who had developed Mel Fisher's first magnetometer years before, had greatly improved the device. It was now more sensitive than ever and reported hits over much greater distances.

Fisher also equipped some of his boats with sonar detection equipment. "Sonar" is an acronym for *so*und *na*vigation *r*anging. A sonar transmitter sends out sound waves. When the sound waves strike a submerged object, they bounce back. By interpreting the reflected sound waves, it is possible to tell the size of the object and where it is located. The navy uses sonar in seeking out enemy submarines.

Although sonar can tell the size of an object and where it is located, it can't identify it. The object might be an ancient wreck, or it might be a coral reef; sonar can't tell the difference between the two. But on Fisher's boats, sonar provided important supplemental information.

Another advance, one that to Fisher was of even greater importance than sonar, is what is known as the Del Norte Navigation System. This equipment replaced the use of theodolites.

Del Norte transmitters would be placed in two towers. Their microwave signals were picked up on the search boat by a receiver that produced a readout giving the boat's distance from each tower. This enabled the captain to quickly determine the position of his boat. He could, in fact, pinpoint his location within a distance of three feet, and this within a search area that might cover several square miles. Once a hit was recorded on the chart, the captain could bring the boat back to the exact spot the next day, the next week, or years later.

"Del Norte produced a revolution in our mapping and search techniques," said Duncan Mathewson. He compared its development and use to the introduction of the mailbox and magnetometer years before.

When the diving season began in the spring of 1985, Kane went back to Hawk Channel to try to pick up the trail once more.

Mel's bank account was shrinking again. He knew that unless he made a major find soon, he would be unable to keep his divers working. He decided to assign two other boats besides the *Dauntless* to work Kane's line: the *Saba Rock* and the *Hatteras*. It was a shot in the dark, Mel figured.

Little happened in April, but in May the trail got very hot. The *Saba Rock* found a ballast stone. A bit bigger than a softball, the stone weighed twenty pounds. To Duncan Mathewson, the stone, which stretched the trail even farther to the southeast, was additional evidence that they were drawing closer to the *Atocha*. Then the *Saba Rock* found some barrel hoops, the *Dauntless* found a spike, and the *Saba Rock* found another ballast stone.

All three boats continued to press ahead. But for several days, they dug only empty holes.

Then, suddenly, at the end of May, Susan Nelson, a diver from the *Saba Rock*, discovered what she would later say looked like a "piece of yellow plastic" lying on the ocean floor. Gold. She began picking up gold bars one after another.

When Mel heard the news, he jumped into a speedboat and hurried to the site. He put on scuba gear and joined the *Saba Rock* divers. While several of the divers recovered gold bars from the bottom, all Mel managed to find was an iron nail.

The cache included thirteen gold bars, four hundred and fourteen silver coins, and four beautifully decorated pieces of gold jewelry in which a total of sixteen emeralds had been mounted. That was all. It was not the *Atocha*. The finds seemed to have been the contents of a single treasure chest. The chest itself had disintegrated.

After that discovery and, later, the finding of a small cannon, the trail turned cold again. No one made a significant find for a week. Then two weeks. Then a month. The divers' morale dipped.

Earlier magnetometer surveys had produced several hits to the southeast of where the *Dauntless* was now working. Sonar surveys had confirmed the magnetometer's findings. Mel told Kane to take the *Dauntless* into that area.

It was probably the best advice Mel had ever given his son. On Wednesday, July 17, divers from the *Dauntless*, checking one of the magnetometer's hits, made a spectacular find. It included hundreds of silver coins, ballast stones, and copper ingots. The next day, divers brought up more of the same, plus magnificent pieces of silverware.

"How about that!" said an excited Mel Fisher. "I think we've really found it this time."

But Duncan Mathewson was not ready to agree. Important pieces of the puzzle were still missing. Where were the hundreds of silver ingots that had been carried aboard the *Atocha*? Where were the chests of coins? Where were all those olive jars? And what about the ballast stones and the ship's timbers?

On Friday, July 18, Mel visited the *Dauntless*. He and Kane took sonar readings all around the boat, pinpointing the spots that seemed to have the most potential. An especially good reading was located about two hundred feet in front of Kane's boat. Kane said he would check it out the next morning. Mel returned to Key West.

Saturday, July 20, 1985, was hot, without any breeze. A storm was gathering force to the south. Kane Fisher and the crew of the *Dauntless* kept watching the sky for the first signs of it.

Kane had anchored the *Dauntless* over a spot where he had obtained magnetometer and sonar readings. He blasted the site with the *Dauntless*'s mailboxes. Two divers, Andy Matroci and Greg Wareham, went down to see what the mailboxes might have revealed. Visibility was good: almost thirty feet.

Matroci swam into the crater that Kane had dug. Along its sloping sides, he suddenly came upon scattered silver coins. He fanned the sand away with his hands. More coins came into view, hundreds of them.

Meanwhile, Wareham had gone on ahead. In one hand he held a metal detector. A dark mass loomed up in front of him. Wareham thought it might be a coral reef. Spiny lobsters were crawling about it. Tropical fish were darting all around. Wareham passed the detector's search coil over the mound. His earphones came alive with sound. Wareham knew immediately that the mound wasn't coral. He looked more closely. It was a solid mass of silver bars and coins. Then he saw timbers, the remains of a ship's hull. He knew then that the long search was over. He had found what was left of the *Atocha*.

Wareham waved Matroci over. The two stared at the treasure pile, hugged one another, then sped to the surface. As Matroci burst out of the water, he screamed to the crew members aboard the *Dauntless*, "It's here! It's the main pile! We're sitting on silver bars."

It was indeed the main pile. It was the "mother lode" to other divers, and the "main hull section" to Duncan Mathewson and his archaeologists. It was found on Saturday, July 20, 1985. It was ten years to the day after the *Northwind* had capsized, bringing death to Dirk and Angel Fisher and diver Rick Gage. It was Mel Fisher's sixteenth year of searching for a ship that had sunk 363 years before. The *Atocha* rested in fifty-four feet of water, within one foot of the water depth recorded by Gaspar de Vargas during his attempt to salvage it in 1622.

Kane Fisher and sister Taffi celebrate the discovery of the *Atocha*. (Pat Clyne)

Aboard the *Dauntless*, Kane Fisher radioed Treasure Salvors' headquarters in Key West. "You can throw away your charts," he shouted into the microphone. "We've found it! We've found it!"

Fisher himself did not hear the good news right away. He was on a shopping expedition, buying a new mask, fins, and other diving equipment. But others in Key West who happened to be tuned to the *Dauntless*'s radio transmissions heard Kane's report. The word spread fast. Local radio stations interrupted their regular program with the news. Townspeople began to converge on the Treasure Salvors headquarters.

Fisher was on his way back to the office when he learned what had happened. Dozens of people ran up to him, shook his hand and clapped him on the back, and offered him their congratulations. "Fantabulous," he kept saying. "Fantabulous."

Meanwhile, aboard the *Dauntless* everyone wanted to go

Fisher's salvage boats cluster at the *Atocha* site; (left to right) the *Virgalona*, *Swordfish*, and *Dauntless*. (Pat Clyne)

down and take a look. Even crew members without scuba equipment went into the water, snorkeling down for a quick glimpse of the mound of stacked silver bars and the ghostly timbers.

It was too late for Fisher to go to the site that day, but he arrived early the next morning. He could hardly believe his eyes. There were boats anchored everywhere. Dozens had tied up to the *Dauntless*, and he had to climb over two or three of them to get aboard the salvage vessel. As he clambered onto the deck, scores of news photographers and television cameramen recorded the scene. They were all shouting directions at once.

Salvage work had already begun. Divers from the *Dauntless* were going down and loading the big bars of silver into plastic milk crates or supermarket shopping carts with the wheels removed. After the containers were hoisted onto the deck of the *Dauntless*, the bars were removed, then stacked in piles.

When Fisher saw the piles of silver, he worried that the *Dauntless* might sink under their weight. Several other of his boats had arrived by this time, so Fisher ordered that some of the bars be transferred to the *Hatteras*, *Virgalona*, *Swordfish*, *Saba Rock*, and *Magruder*.

At last Fisher got a chance to put on flippers, mask, and tank and go below. In the silent underwater world, he stared at what remained of the stack of silver bars, the clumps of coins in chest shapes, and priceless artifacts.

When he went back aboard, he sat quietly for a while, puffing a cigarette, seemingly unmindful of the bedlam about him. "I knew it was there all along," he said. "It *had* to be there."

Duncan Mathewson and his archaeological team were al-

Aboard the *Dauntless*, Fisher examines a diver's find. (Pat Clyne)

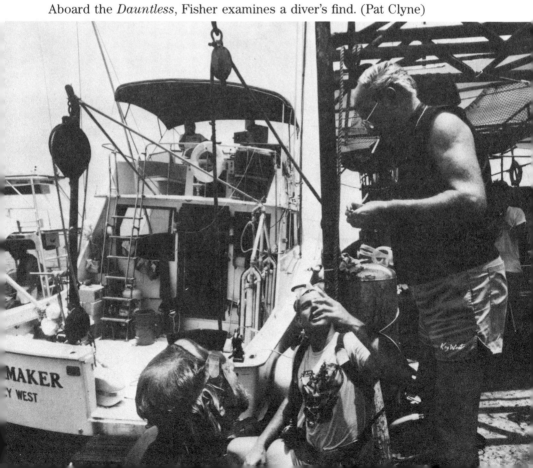

Archaeologists carefully numbered and photographed each of the *Atocha*'s timbers. (Pat Clyne)

ready at work. They began laying down a 150-foot baseline through the center of the site. They planned to fix measuring tapes along the line at various intervals. This system would enable the archaeologists and divers to pinpoint each artifact on the site map. Mathewson also started numbering each of the timbers and mapping them in position.

Mathewson urged the boat captains and divers to stop using the mailboxes. When they blasted away, the timbers quivered and the pile of silver ingots rocked back and forth. Mathewson had visions of the entire site being demolished before it could be mapped and photographed.

The divers showed little willingness to cooperate. They wanted to continue to bring up ingots and other treasure. "We're not concerned with archaeology like you are," one diver told Mathewson. "We're treasure divers."

Another pointed to the name TREASURE SALVORS on the side of the boat. "That's our name," he said, "and that's what we do."

The problem was worse the next morning. Mathewson and two members of his archaeological team were at the bottom laying the base line, when suddenly they were engulfed in a whirlwind of sand. Kane Fisher had decided to "blow" with the *Dauntless*'s mailboxes.

Mathewson was enraged. He couldn't believe that one of the most important archaeological sites in the Americas was being blasted by a propwash from a salvage boat.

He hurried to the surface, climbed the ladder of the *Dauntless*, and, still wearing his scuba gear, stormed into the wheelhouse to confront Kane. "Stop those blowers right now," Mathewson shouted, "or you'll destroy the whole site."

"Your father won't go down in history as the man who found the *Atocha*," he continued, "he'll be remembered as the man who destroyed it." Kane reached over and switched off the *Dauntless*'s engines.

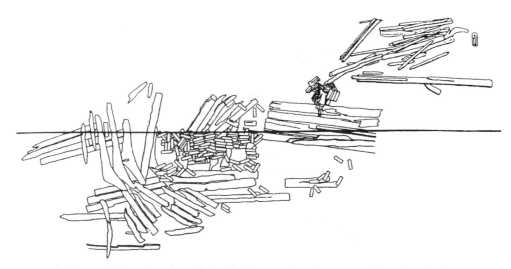

Archaeologist's drawing of *Atocha*'s lower hull structure showing timbers and silver bars (small rectangles). (Treasure Salvors)

Shortly after, Mel arrived. Mathewson got him to agree that none of the boat crews would use their mailboxes over the mother lode. Instead, divers would dig with hand-held airlifts and then only when the artifacts could be recorded and mapped as they were uncovered. From that day on, site operations were conducted in a scientific way.

In the weeks and months that followed, the site yielded tens of millions of dollars in treasure. Before the end of 1985, Fisher's divers hauled up 950 silver bars and 140,000 silver coins. Most of the coins were welded together in chest-shaped forms, the result of the erosion that had taken place during 363 years in salt water.

During 1985, 166 gold bars, disks, and other bits and pieces were recovered. Many of them bore tax stamps, carat stamps, or foundry marks. Sixty-seven gold coins and fifteen gold chains were found.

R. Duncan Mathewson examines chest-shaped mass of coins found at *Atocha* site. (Pat Clyne)

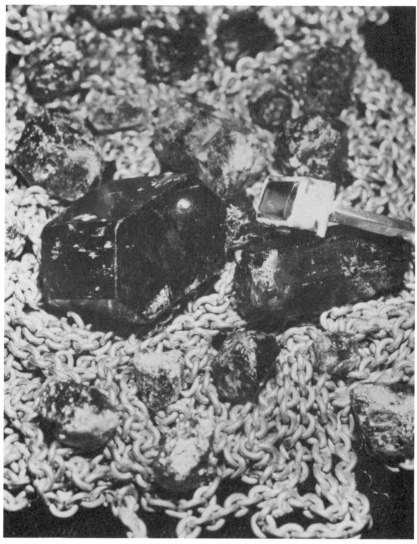
Besides silver and gold, *Atocha* site proved rich in emeralds. (Pat Clyne)

Close to a thousand artifacts cast in precious metal were found at the site that year. These included silver plates, cups, bowls, spoons, and candlesticks.

The site also yielded emeralds. In 1985 alone, divers found 315 of the precious blazing green stones. Some were tiny; it took more than a dozen of them to cover a dime. But others were of remarkable size, as big as large gumdrops. The biggest, the size and shape of a small Tootsie Roll, weighed 77.13 carats. Gem specialists identified the emeralds as having come from the famed Muzo mine region of Colombia.

Mel had once heard that a huge shipment of emeralds had been smuggled aboard the *Atocha* not long before the vessel left Havana. While he had no evidence to support the story, Mel repeated it often. Now it seemed the tale might be true after all.

Before fall turned to winter in 1985, and with strong winds beginning to lash the site, archaeologists covered the timbers with sheets of heavy plastic, weighting them with sand and stones. The sheets were used to protect the remains of the *Atocha* until the spring and the return of mild weather, when recovery work could be resumed.

Emeralds recovered by Fisher's divers come close to filling a quart jar.
(Pat Clyne)

13

Treasures of the Mainland Fleet

I n the year that followed, Fisher's divers continued to recover more gold, silver, and jewels from the *Atocha*. And emeralds. In 1986 alone, more than 2,500 emeralds were discovered.

Fisher estimated that the treasure that had been found through 1985 had a value of about $130 million. Altogether, the sum may one day total as much as $200 million, and some treasure seekers claim that it could eventually reach twice that amount.

Whatever figure is used, one thing is certain: No other treasure find comes close to equaling that of the *Atocha*. As one diver put it, "What we've found on the *Atocha* makes every other treasure site look like bus fare."

But to many, the real riches of the *Atocha* are not represented by gold, silver, or precious jewels. The ship's remains and the hundreds of thousands of recovered artifacts are proving to be a scientific treasure of unrivaled importance. By studying these objects, archaeologists and historians are beginning to get new insights concerning Spanish conquests in the New World.

Such study begins on the salvage boats. Each boat crew includes one or more individuals who are trained in archaeo-

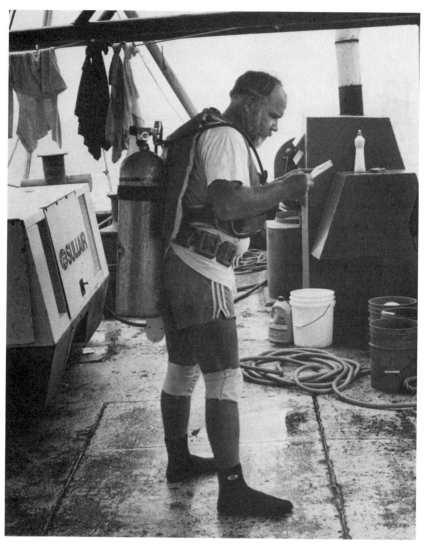

Aboard the salvage boat *Magruder,* marine archaeologist John Dorwin prepares for a dive to the *Atocha* site. (George Sullivan)

logical research. As soon as an object is spotted on the ocean bottom, it is tagged with a coded identification number. An archaeological mapper pinpoints each object on a site map. In some cases, objects are photographed or drawn by an artist before being moved.

Jerry Cash, an artist and a mapmaker, checks equipment before a dive to sketch *Atocha*'s timbers. (George Sullivan)

After recovered objects are unloaded at Treasure Salvors's pier in Key West, they are taken to the sprawling archaeological laboratory on the third floor of Fisher's headquarters building. Dozens of archaeologists and laboratory assistants work there. Specialists in seventeenth-century Spanish coins, in jewelry, pottery, and ship-building techniques participate in the studies.

As a first step, programmers log each object into the Treasure Salvors's computer system. Each is digitally photographed and assigned a bar code, which is similar to the Universal Product Code symbol found on most supermarket products. When passed over a laser, the symbol can call up the computer listing of the object along with its digitized photo.

Most objects made of metal require special treatment. Iron artifacts, for example, are often encased in marine growth. What can result is a hard, shapeless mass, called a conglomerate. Archaeologists sometimes begin work on a conglomerate by x-raying it. This enables them to see the shape of the object buried inside.

Removing the encrusted material is a slow process. It sometimes takes hours of gentle hammering and careful chipping followed by delicate picking with instruments that resemble the tools a dentist uses.

Heavy marine growth coats an anchor fluke. (George Sullivan)

Lab assistant works to restore what remains of a gold-tinted silver plate. (George Sullivan)

One of the largest conglomerates was discovered at the site of the *Santa Margarita*. Roughly the size of an office desk, it weighed about two tons. When it arrived aboard the salvage boat at Fisher's pier in Key West, a crane hoisted the bulky mass to a flatbed truck that carried it to the archaeological lab. Once work began on the conglomerate, cannonball after cannonball began to appear. The total number eventually reached 250. Four silver coins, some crystal beads, fragments of glass, and a bone—not human—were also found within the big clump.

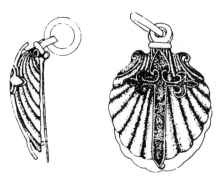

Gold pendant in scallop shape was found within pear-shaped clump of coins. (Treasure Salvors)

A pear-shaped conglomerate from the *Santa Margarita* seemed to be made entirely of silver coins. But toward the center of the mass, the glint of gold suddenly appeared. Working carefully with small hand tools, an archaeologist removed the black crust that surrounded the gold object. It turned out to be a gold pendant that once must have dangled from a gold chain or necklace. It was in the shape of a scallop shell.

When the pendant was opened, delicate engraving could be

A plaster reproduction of a chest-shaped conglomerate of coins. (George Sullivan)

seen on the inside surfaces. The top shell had a lacy design through which the initials YE showed. The bottom shell bore the cross of Santiago de Compostela, who was the seventeenth-century symbol of the knighthood of St. James.

Other conglomerates found at the *Atocha* site were composed of many thousands of silver coins fused together in a treasure-chest shape. A specialist first duplicated each coin mass in plaster. This assured that there would be a permanent and accurate record of what each "chest" looked like.

After more than three hundred years in the sea, silver coins are black and lumpy with encrustations. Chemical treatment makes them shine almost like new.

Silver coins are black and lumpy when found. (Pat Clyne)

Clumps of coins are broken apart. Then the individual coins are clipped to metal rods and bathed in a mild acid solution. "The acid is something like vinegar," said Tony Kopp, who headed the coin restoration project for Treasure Salvors. "You

Tony Kopp prepares to dip encrusted coins in a chemical bath. (George Sullivan)

can put your fingers in it; it won't hurt you. But it's effective in removing some of the deposits that coat the coin."

Silver coins are critically damaged by the salt in sea water. It turns the silver to silver chloride. "The salt penetrates to almost the center of the coin," said Tony Kopp, "right through the metal."

A process known as electrolytic reduction extracts the salt. The coins are suspended from their metal rods in a solution of caustic soda and water. While they hang there, electric current is passed through each one. After twenty-four hours, the silver chloride has been removed.

After the coins are taken from the electrolytic bath, they're put in a barrel tumbler with small steel balls. They tumble for ten to twenty minutes. When they're removed from the tumbler, then rinsed in clear water and dried, the coins are bright and shining once more.

After chemical treatment, coins are bright and shiny. (George Sullivan)

"Every so often I come upon a counterfeit coin," said Kopp. "Maybe one coin in a thousand is a fake. Counterfeit coins are made of lead. They look different; they feel different; they even sound different. A silver coin gives off a nice, melodious ring when you tap it with something, like a ballpoint pen. But a lead coin has no ring."

Counterfeiting wasn't the only method of deception involving coins. There was also coin clipping. A person would snip a tiny piece from the edge of each of a thousand or so coins. After all that snipping, the result would be a few ounces of silver to be melted down and sold.

Another method of fraud was to put several hundred coins in a heavy leather bag. The bag would then be smashed against the ground again and again. After several hours, a few ounces of valuable silver dust would accumulate at the bottom of the bag.

After the coins are restored to their original brilliance, they are carefully sorted and graded. At one time, more than two thousand silver coins were being restored daily at Fisher's laboratory.

Each coin carries the coat of arms of whichever Spanish monarch happened to be in power at the time the coin was minted. The reverse side presents images of lions and castles. These represent the Spanish kingdoms of Castile and León.

Mint marks indicate where each coin was made. Silver coins from the *Atocha* were made at mints in Mexico, Lima, Potosí, and La Plata.

A handful of coins represent the Santa Fé de Bogotá mint. While the existence of this mint has been known to coin experts for many years, the *Atocha* coins are believed to be the first ever recovered from it.

N. Neil Harris, editor of *The Numismatist*, a magazine devoted to the study and collection of coins, has called the *Atocha* coins "one of the most important discoveries of all time." Study of the hoard continues under the direction of Sandy McKinney, Treasure Salvors's coin expert.

A large section of the archaeological laboratory is devoted to the cleaning and restoring of silver artifacts, such as cups, pitchers, plates, and candlesticks.

Some of the silver artifacts demonstrate how the Spanish and Indian cultures blended in the New World. The center of one plate, for example, displays the image of a bird with a shield. This is a fairly typical Spanish design of the time. But about the plate's edge there are images of Indians involved in such activities as planting corn and using llamas as pack animals.

"European silversmiths came to South America," archaeologist Jim Sinclair explains, "and used native craftsmen as their helpers. That's why some objects reflect cultural and artistic roots in both the Old and New Worlds."

Sinclair adds: "Some of the pieces we've recovered from the *Atocha* are unlike anything ever produced in Spain or Portugal—or anywhere else in the world."

Not only silversmiths but goldsmiths were active in the New World. But only a relatively few examples of their craftsmanship have been preserved, since the Spanish conquerors frequently melted down Indian gold objects and shipped the gold back to Spain in the form of bars or ingots.

One of the most fascinating gold objects found at the *Atocha* site is a "poison cup" or, rather, an "antipoison cup." It was discovered by Kim Fisher. Decorated with images of a lion, a rabbit, and fire-breathing dragons, the cup is an object of rare beauty. Sculpted dragons form its two handles. The inside rim is ringed with settings that once held precious stones. It could only have belonged to a person of very high rank.

The cup had an unusual role to play. A wire frame within the

Rare "anti-poison" cup found by Kim Fisher. (Pat Clyne)

bowl held what was known as a bezoar, a small, stonelike mass that forms in the digestive tract of goats and llamas. Bezoars were highly prized by royalty in the Middle Ages because it was believed that they were capable of absorbing arsenic. Thus, if an arsenic-poisoned drink were to be poured into the cup and the bezoar was in place, it would soak up the arsenic and the drinker would escape being poisoned.

The protective power of the bezoar, several of which were found by Fisher's divers, was no myth. There is now scientific proof that arsenic bonds chemically with certain substances contained in the bezoar.

Pottery survives in sea water, and thus a great deal of study involving the treasure galleons has focused on the pieces, called shards, and complete vessels that have been recovered. This research is revealing the techniques and methods used by seventeenth-century potters in making vessels of a wide variety of shapes and sizes.

The pottery finds have included three huge intact jars, each capable of holding from twenty-five to thirty gallons of liquid. John Dorwin, senior archaeologist for fieldwork and laboratory analysis, believes that vessels of this type, called *tinajas*, were placed about the ship to provide water for the crew and passengers. They thus served the same purpose as a water fountain does today.

Huge jars, called *tinajas*, are believed to have been used to provide water for *Atocha*'s crew and passengers. (George Sullivan)

Tens of thousands of pottery pieces have been found. Sometimes archaeologists recover so many pieces of the same vessel that they are able to reconstruct it. This process is like putting a jigsaw puzzle together.

Most pottery shards have a special characteristic that aids in sorting and reconstruction. Rim pieces, circular in shape, are different from body pieces. Handle parts are slim and curved; base pieces are thick and relatively heavy.

Most of the pottery fragments and complete vessels found at the *Atocha* and *Santa Margarita* sites are olive jars of various sizes. Olive jars initially carried only olives. But through the years they came to be used to transport or store a wide variety of foodstuffs. A ship such as the *Atocha* may have had as many as a thousand olive jars aboard. "They were the five-gallon utility can of the era," says R. Duncan Mathewson.

By early 1987, more than one hundred olive-jar rims had been recovered at the *Atocha* site. Ten of the rims have unusual identification marks. Little is known about such markings, and they have become the subject of special study.

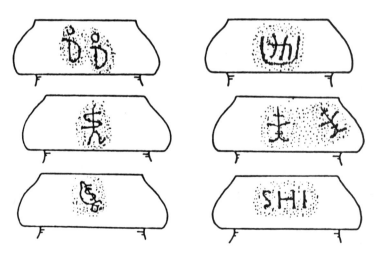

Some olive-jar rims have unusual markings. (Treasure Salvors)

The timbers that formed the *Atocha*'s lower hull structure have been given special treatment. Late in 1986, Mel Fisher donated forty of them, each about twenty feet in length, to Florida Keys Community College in Key West. The timbers were placed in a salt-water diving pit forty feet deep, where they will be studied by marine archaeologists.

"The timbers are the largest single collection of remains from a Spanish galleon," says John Dorwin. "And in terms of construction of such a galleon, very little is known." Dorwin predicts that the timbers will reveal important information about the architecture and construction of seventeenth-century ships.

By 1987, several studies of the artifacts recovered from the *Atocha* and *Santa Margarita* were well under way. "But we've got years of work ahead of us," says R. Duncan Mathewson. "It may be another decade or more before we're through deciphering the ship's construction and studying the artifacts. When we're finished, I think we'll be able to rewrite the history of the period. What could be more exciting than that?"

As for the recovered treasure, most of it has been distributed to Fisher's associates at Treasure Salvors, his divers and boat captains, and to the more than one thousand investors who backed his search for it. In the division, Fisher himself received two of the most valued pieces of treasure—two chests of silver coins still intact. The chests have been described as priceless.

Some of what has been recovered is now on exhibit on the first floor of Fisher's headquarters in Key West. Tourists often line up outside, waiting to buy tickets. Inside they see stunning gold bars, stacks of heavy silver ingots, ornate gold jewelry, and some of the more than three thousand emeralds divers have found. People speak in hushed tones as they file through the exhibit areas, almost as if there were something religious about the treasure.

"One thing I get a kick out of is the busloads of kids we get," Fisher once said. "History was once boring to them, but when they see this exhibit they get excited. I love seeing that!"

Fisher has often said that as much as half of the *Atocha's* treasure may still be lying on the ocean bottom. It spilled out of the ship's hull as the galleon broke apart and sank.

Fisher, however, has no plans to search for it. Late in 1986, he sold the salvage rights to the *Atocha* and *Santa Margarita* to a group of investors.

The sale made Fisher a millionaire many times over. But he is still interested in treasure hunting. There are several sites he wants to investigate. One is Corrigan's Wreck, a stretch of ocean floor off Vero Beach, Florida. "We think there are twelve ships there," Fisher has said. "They're Spanish ships that sank in a hurricane in 1715, and they are supposed to be filled with gold."

Fisher often tells people that the best wrecks are yet to be found. Even if that should happen to be true, it is likely that most of them will remain hidden by sand and water. They'll remain hidden until another person such as Mel Fisher comes along, someone with Fisher's daring and persistence, his spirit of adventure, and above all, his willingness to pursue a dream as romantic as sunken treasure.

Sources

Much of the material in this book is based on interviews with men and women representing Treasure Salvors, Inc. These include R. Duncan Mathewson, Archaeological Director; John Dorwin, Senior Archaeologist in Charge of Field Work and Laboratory Analysis; and Jim Sinclair, Director of Conservation and Preservation; as well as boat captains, divers, and technical experts.

The author also relied on many books for historical background. Chief among them were:

Treasure of the Atocha, by R. Duncan Mathewson (Pisces Books, 1986)

The Search for the Atocha, by Eugene Lyon (Florida Classics Library, 1985)

Treasure, by Robert Daley (Pocket Books, 1986)

The Portable Prescott: The Rise and Decline of the Spanish Empire, selected and edited by Irwin R. Blacker (The Viking Press, 1963)

The Golden Century of Spain, 1501–1621, by R. Trevor Davies (Harper Torchbooks, 1965)

Index